HIS MAJESTY'S TEMPORARY BRIDE

BY

ANNIE WEST

MILLS & BOON

First published in Great Britain 2017
by Mills & Boon, an imprint of HarperCollins*Publishers*
1 London Bridge Street, London, SE1 9GF

Large Print edition 2018

© 2017 Annie West

ISBN: 978-0-263-07336-2

MIX
Paper from
responsible sources
FSC C007454

This book is produced from independently certified FSC™
paper to ensure responsible forest management. For more
information visit www.harpercollins.co.uk/green.

Printed and bound in Great Britain
by CPI Group (UK) Ltd, Croydon, CR0 4YY

This is my 30th book
for Harlequin Mills & Boon!
Thirty stories would not have been possible
without the support of my fabulous editorial
team in London and all the other staff who
work hard to ensure my published books
are the best they can be. My family, who are
gracious and supportive despite my mind
often being elsewhere. My writing friends,
who know how to celebrate and motivate
and make even the tough days fun.

And above all you, my readers, who enjoy the
books and encourage me to keep dreaming.

Thank you so very much!

PROLOGUE

CAT VAULTED OVER the low wall, her blood singing at the sheer joy of running *parcours*. Her breathing was fast but her movements measured as she and Paolo raced through the abandoned warehouse.

She vaulted, then made a tic-tac of her feet on a wall as she built momentum and leapt, grabbing the edge of an empty skylight. Swinging, Cat hauled herself up and over the edge. It was there Paolo passed her. She was fast and agile but he beat her hands-down in upper body strength.

With a whoop he was away, across the roof to clatter down an empty stairwell while she raced to draw close. Bounding off stairs, walls and a balustrade, she'd almost caught him when they reached the perimeter fence.

'Mine today,' he gasped.

Cat nodded, bracing hands on knees. Her ponytail swung over her shoulder as she breathed deep. 'That *passe muraille* of yours was faultless.'

He grinned. 'Something for you to aim for?'

She punched his arm. 'Almost up to my standard.'

They headed for the exit. 'Same time next week?'

'I may have a job out of town. I'll call.'

He nodded and unlocked his car. 'You need a lift?'

Cat shook her head. 'No. I'm heading to the gym.' The outwardly dilapidated but excellent gym they used was around the corner. She wanted to check on the kids she'd been coaching after school. They were troubled teens, like she'd been. But they showed promise and while she was between jobs she enjoyed being with them.

She turned into the dog-leg alley shortcut, head full of teenagers and their prickly pride. Which was no excuse for the few seconds it took to scope danger. The shiny limo was out of place in this part of New York. But it was the tall guy with the bulge under his jacket, peeling away from the wall, she should have noticed instantly.

He moved fast as a professional. But so was she. When he reached for her she ducked, grabbed his wrist and used his forward momentum to crash him to the ground. Knee between his shoulder blades, she took his gun.

'Ms Dubois!'

She turned, hearing the man beneath her groan

as her knee swivelled. Standing in the doorway of the limo was a slim man in a dark suit, eyes wide.

'Ms Dubois, please. I only want to talk.' The air expelled from her lungs in a rush. Because the man didn't speak English but the distinctive patois of her native tongue—a modified version of French. Alarm bells rang, leaving her more rather than less alert.

'Who are you?' She eased back, giving the guy beneath her room to breathe, keeping a hand locked on his wrist.

The man at the limo stepped closer. 'I'm the St Gallan ambassador to the US. I'm here with a job offer. If I may show you my credentials?' Slowly he approached and Cat read his ID. It was genuine.

Tucking the gun into her waistband, she rose. 'If you want to talk, why send *him*?' She gestured to the big man clambering to his feet.

The ambassador grimaced. 'I was told you might not welcome an approach from St Galla and I needed to be sure you'd listen. His instructions were to bring you to the car so we could talk.'

His bodyguard straightened, rolling his shoulder to test it and nodded. 'Tactical mistake. I knew you were one of us but I didn't expect...' He shrugged, then winced.

'I'm not interested in a job in St Galla.' She'd left her island home at eighteen after her mother's funeral. The place held nothing for her after she lost the one person who'd ever loved her, the only one *she'd* loved.

The ambassador nodded. 'There's someone who could change your mind. The Prime Minister is waiting.'

Cat's eyes darted to the limo's tinted windows.

'A long-distance call. Allow me to offer you the privacy of my car while you talk.'

Angry and confused, Cat was in no mood to comply. But curiosity won and she found herself alone in the vehicle, looking at a screen and the thin, clever face of the St Gallan Prime Minister, Monsieur Barthe. He looked shocked.

'By God, you *are* like her! I saw the photos but...'

Cat's skin crawled. That feeling of a thousand ants swarming. She hadn't felt it in years but it was back with a vengeance, dredging a lifetime's painful memories.

'Who are you talking about?' As if she didn't know.

'Princess Amelie.' He shook his head. 'The similarity is astonishing.'

Cat remained silent. She'd learned there was nothing she could say. As a kid, the taunts and snide accusations had grown unbearable. She'd tried turning the other cheek, ignoring them, even fighting back when the bullies got physical. All that had got her was more trouble. On the upside it led to an interest in martial arts that had eventually been her key to escape.

She set her jaw, hating the feeling of powerlessness after all these years and a continent of distance. It was as if ten years had vanished in an instant, all she'd achieved a mirage.

'Ms Dubois, I have an important, confidential assignment for you.'

'I'm always discreet.' As a bodyguard to the famous it was a necessity. 'But I'm not interested.'

'This is for your country.'

Her country could go hang. She hadn't been able to shake its dust soon enough. Her first eighteen years had been torment, defending herself and her mother's reputation endlessly in public. Then at home, watching the man she'd had to call father grind her mother down.

'I'm still not interested.'

'Even though Lambis Evangelos recommended you?'

Lambis? He was the best in the business. His

company *ran* the best in the business. They'd met in Chicago when she worked with Afra, the superstar singer. Cat had been pleased at his interest, his offer of an open door if ever she wanted work.

But to work in St Galla? She shuddered. 'I suggest you find someone else.'

Shrewd eyes surveyed her. The next question would be *why* she wouldn't return to her homeland. As if she'd share that with anyone. The only people who'd known the truth about her were dead. She wasn't about to let anyone else in on her sordid secret.

'There are plenty of other bodyguards.' Though she prided herself that those who employed her asked for her again and again, particularly women who felt more comfortable with a female shadowing them.

His voice dropped. 'We need your special…attributes. Mr Evangelos suggested you if we ever needed a body double for Princess Amelie.'

Cat sat back, pulse racing. 'She's in danger?' Her voice was inexplicably husky. She'd never met the Princess yet still she felt a connection.

'Not…danger. Though the situation is delicate.'

'What situation?'

'The Princess is…away.' He paused as if choosing his words. 'We're not sure when she'll return. Meantime it's vital she appear at a small palace reception. This event *must* go ahead, for the nation and the Princess herself.'

Cat stared. 'You want me to impersonate Princess Amelie? You can't be serious!' She'd grown up being compared with the Princess. The woman was charming, elegant, graceful, accomplished in ways Cat wasn't. She wore jewels and formal gowns. Cat was allergic to high heels and had never worn a full-length dress in her life.

'Deadly serious.' His tone chilled her and again that shiver of preternatural connection, of anxiety, passed through her. 'You wouldn't have to face anyone who knows the Princess well. All you have to do is make an appearance, chat a little, then withdraw.'

'It's not possible.'

'Not even for a very generous settlement?' Monsieur Barthe named a sum that made her goggle.

'You can't be serious.' Shock stretched her voice.

His mouth tightened. 'Completely. Money is no object.'

Cat blinked. With that money she could achieve her dream. Bodyguard work had been good to her but she couldn't do it for ever. Already she wondered how long her knee would hold up long-term. Last year she'd been injured saving Afra from a car driven by a crazed stalker. It had been a long slog to get back to something like her previous fitness.

Cat had no other qualifications, no career path. But working with kids, diverting their negative energy into physical endeavours and a positive outlook—*that* she could do. Developing a centre either in the wilderness or in a city gym devoted specifically to kids—she'd give so much to achieve that. For the kids and herself.

'Half the money in advance and half on completion.'

She jerked her head up, meeting steely eyes that had read her momentary lapse.

Cat shook her head. 'I might look superficially like her, but I'm no princess. Everyone would know.'

'Not a problem. You'd stay at the palace in advance of the event to be tutored in everything you need to know.' He paused, surveying her set features. 'Look on it as your chance to see how the other half lives.'

Cat stared as the words insinuated themselves into her brain. How often in childhood had she wondered what it was like to be Amelie? To live the cosseted life of a rich, beloved child, adored by her father and the nation? It had been a fantasy she'd retreated to when reality grew unbearable. She'd put it behind her years ago, yet to her amazement shreds of that yearning still lingered.

'I'll double the fee.'

Cat goggled. The amount was ridiculously huge. What on earth was going on?

'The Princess…is she safe?' Again, that sixth sense niggle of concern.

'I'm not in a position to say. But you'll help her enormously by doing this.'

Cat didn't need Princess Amelie's gratitude. She could get by without the money, even though it represented more than she'd earn in the next several years. It shouldn't matter if it brought her dream to reality.

Returning to the country of her birth would betray the vow she'd made at eighteen never to look back.

Yet something stopped her refusal. The possibility that Amelie genuinely needed her? Or that the bastard half-sister finally had a chance to discover what life would have been like if she'd been born legitimate? To experience the life she might have had?

No, it was far more than that. This wasn't curiosity to see how the other half lived. It was a desire, deep down in her secret self, to connect with the family she'd never known. To find a way to meet her sibling. For years she'd told herself no good could come of connecting with her royal relations, yet still that yearning remained. To belong.

Cat cleared her throat, hating the tug of emotion turning her voice hoarse. Hating the neediness. She'd thought she'd conquered it years ago.

Maybe this is your chance to do that.

And still that snaking anxiety for the half-sister she'd never met. 'Send me a contract to consider.'

His smile told her he knew he'd won. 'You won't regret it, Ms Dubois.'

She already did. But she had to do this and silence once and for all the voices of her murky past.

CHAPTER ONE

ALEX STRETCHED, STARING out over the azure depths of the Mediterranean.

He hadn't wanted to come. If he'd been able to avoid the celebration in St Galla he'd have done it, especially as his mother had stitched up a half-baked proposal that Princess Amelie would make him the perfect bride.

He was only thirty-two, had only been King for three years. He had more important things to grapple with than marrying, no matter what his advisers thought.

Giving up a career he loved to rule Bengaria hadn't been in his plans. Alex's fists clenched as he leaned on the gleaming rail of the yacht.

It should have been his cousin, Stefan, on the throne. Except for the accident that had snuffed out his life and propelled Alex's father into his place. His late and unlamented father. The man who'd almost bankrupted Bengaria in the years he'd been Stefan's Regent and later the King. The man whose chicanery and double-dealing had milked the nation almost to a standstill, leaving Alex to haul an economic nightmare out of the red and into the black.

No wonder everyone wanted Alex to marry Amelie. St Galla was wealthy and could help Bengaria, even though he was hopeful his country was beginning to recover now.

He sighed and forked a hand through his hair. He'd only agreed to the visit because of his mother. She'd suffered long and hard through her marriage. Alex had at least escaped his father's control by leaving Bengaria and pursuing a career as a pilot. She'd been stuck in a loveless marriage to a despicable man.

A familiar chill rippled down his spine at the thought of his father.

In the circumstances, meeting Amelie, the daughter of his mother's best friend, was little recompense for all she'd put up with. He'd attend the reception to commemorate five hundred years of friendship between their countries then return home and report that Amelie wasn't the woman for him.

Now, with the early sun warming his bare back and the prospect of no civic duties, he felt a lightness he hadn't known since he'd given up flying. These couple of days were his first vacation in three years. Even though he'd spend most of it working from his office on the yacht, it felt like freedom. Temporary but glorious.

He sauntered along the deck, contemplating a dip, when a shout rang out. He swivelled to face the shore.

Another shout. A splash.

Alex narrowed his eyes against the sun's golden dazzle. In the distance he made out a capsized canoe and flailing arms. Another shout and a submerging head.

'George!' He raced along the deck. 'Get the tender! Someone's in trouble.' For the people—two of them—weren't swimming. One floated near the hull of the canoe and a second floundered mere metres from it.

Alex dived, the cool water a shock after the warmth of the sun. He surfaced and powered towards the accident.

How had they capsized in such still waters?

Why weren't they wearing life vests? Obviously they weren't since one was sinking.

Hauling in air, Alex forced himself to concentrate on the quick, hard rhythm of his strokes, forging through the water with a speed that might, he hoped, save a life and hopefully two.

A gurgling cry told him he was close and he stopped to discover he was only metres away.

A third head bobbed in the water but he realised with relief this woman could swim. She held a boy under the chin, propping his face above water as she sliced back through the water towards the canoe.

'You're okay?' he gasped.

Her head lifted and his gaze collided with gleaming green, the colour of mountain meadows.

'We will be,' she said through gritted teeth, 'when he stops fighting me.' The teenager was flailing, one long, thin arm reaching back, grabbing at her head.

Alex moved towards them but she was already disengaging the kid's grasp, telling him firmly but calmly to lie still and let her do the work. Seeing she had things under control, he turned to the canoe where another dark head bobbed precariously low in the water.

Swearing under his breath he raced across, hauling a body up under the arms till the kid started coughing water. No hope of righting the canoe with a dead weight in his hands. Instead he shoved the kid high, so high he lay sprawled over the hull, arms flopping down its other side.

Satisfied he was safe, Alex turned and found the other swimmer had successfully brought the second boy up behind him.

'Let me give you a hand.'

She nodded and told the kid what they were going to do, again in that clear, calm tone. Then she held the canoe steady while Alex hauled him up onto the hull beside his companion.

Alex's chest and shoulders burned from the effort. Both teens were lanky and getting purchase in the water had taken a lot of strength. He grimaced. He needed to get out of the office a whole lot more.

'You'll be okay.' He blinked and realised the woman wasn't reassuring him but the two boys. She'd moved round to the other side of the canoe and was inspecting them.

Alex joined her, relieved to see both kids breathing, albeit in rough gasps.

In the distance he heard a motor start. 'Help's on its way. That's the tender from the yacht.'

She nodded, her attention fixed on the youngsters, and Alex found his gaze dwelling on her high-cut cheekbones, straight nose and plump bow of a mouth. Mermaids were supposed to be beautiful and this one didn't disappoint.

Abruptly she turned her head, catching his stare. Alex felt their gazes mesh, a palpable connection, and wondered if it had been so long since he'd been with a pretty woman that his brain had turned to mush in the interim.

'What?'

'Nothing.' He shook his head. 'It will be easier to transfer them from the other side. I'll go round and help George if you can stay here and reassure them.'

'Of course.' Her voice had a lilt that tugged at something deep inside and told him English wasn't her first language. He wondered how his name would sound on her lips.

Alex swam around the canoe. First her eyes, now her voice. Had it *really* been so long since he'd been with a woman?

He banished the thought as George cut the engine and the pair of them worked to get the kids aboard. Once more his golden-haired mermaid proved quietly efficient, easing their burden.

'Here.' He beckoned her over when the others were aboard the small boat. 'I'll give you a boost up.'

'No need.' She flashed him a smile and his pulse kicked hard.

Number three. First the eyes, then the voice. But that smile surpassed the rest. It turned his cool, capable, impervious mermaid into a beckoning sea sprite. That smile was pure mischief and again he felt that draw in his belly, hard and urgent.

Before Alex knew what she intended, or George could offer her a hand, she planted her hands on the side of the tender and pulled herself up smoothly and easily.

He was treated to a view of neat breasts against a saturated T-shirt, a slim waist, baggy shorts and long, shapely legs of pale gold.

Four. Alex clutched the boat, breathing hard. Despite the cool water, this time his response wasn't belly-deep but lower, stirring his groin. He'd always had a weakness for great legs.

'Want some help?' She leaned out, ready to offer a hand, that smile dancing at the edge of her lips.

In that instant Alex knew if he was still the impulsive guy he'd once been, carefree and unencumbered by a crown, he'd have curled his hand around her neck and tugged her close. He'd have kissed her till she planted those small, capable hands on his chest and begged for more.

And he'd have given it.

'I can manage.' He hauled himself up.

It was as her eyes rounded that he remembered he'd dived naked into the sea. With the yacht's crew on shore leave and only he and George aboard, he hadn't bothered dressing when he woke.

Her gaze stayed low on his body a fraction too long, making his blood surge south in response.

Her eyes flashed to his. 'I'm guessing you weren't expecting company.' Her lips twitched.

Five. Most women he met these days lacked a sense of humour. He missed that. In his old life he'd been part of a close-knit team where humour made a demanding job easier.

'I was thinking about an early morning dip, but not like this.' He was responding way too much to the glint of humour in her bright eyes and the husky edge to her voice.

He moved further into the small boat and stood. Alex was fully aware the movement laid his back and buttocks bare to her gaze—he'd swear he could feel the prickle of her regard right now. But it was better than presenting her with what could too easily turn into a promising erection.

He hunkered down at the side of the boat, motioning for George to start the motor. One of the

kids had a gash on his temple and there was a
first aid kit on the yacht. To his relief though, they
seemed to be improving by the minute.

By the time the five of them were on the yacht
Alex knew they'd be okay. He got the first aid kit
then left it in George's capable hands while he went
below to dry off and dress.

Yet as he tugged on old jeans and a shirt, Alex
could recall exactly how he'd felt when the mermaid's gaze dropped to his chest, lingered a second
and then kept moving to his abdomen and groin.
The prickle under his skin was a prelude to something he could *not* afford to give in to.

The timing was all wrong.

So was the place. The person.

Imagine the complications if he followed his in-
stincts and pursued an affair with her right here,
offshore from the palace! Especially when there
were so many people in both countries promoting
a royal wedding.

Alex shuddered and zipped his jeans. Marriage
was *not* on the agenda.

'There's Alex now,' George said and Cat looked
up. Alex, the owner of the beautiful vintage yacht,
strolled towards them. His gait was loose-hipped

and easy, shoulders back as if he hadn't a care in the world. Definitely the walk of an assured man. One too sexy for his own good.

Fire spiked in her blood as she recalled his lazy, half-lidded expression when she'd seen him naked. The devastatingly attractive way the corners of his mouth curled up, the gleam in those indigo eyes.

She liked a confident man. One assured enough not to bolster his ego at the expense of others.

He was athletic too. That tall body was strong and taut and oh-so attractive, with powerful thighs and sinewy forearms and a classic male outline that tapered from wide shoulders. She had a sudden recollection of the bunch of his rounded, perfect glutes as he'd walked away. Cat forced her attention back to the bandage she was securing.

'There, that should do.'

'Good work, Cat.' George, the yacht's captain, closed the first aid kit.

'Cat?' The lazy drawl was like fingertips dancing down her spine. She told herself it was the breeze cooling her ancient T-shirt against her skin but she feared it was his luscious baritone.

'Alex, this is Cat. Cat, Alex.'

'Nice to meet you... Cat.'

She looked up to read curiosity crinkling his

broad brow. A flare of his nostrils brought that chiselled, patrician nose to life and his dark blue eyes narrowed as he surveyed her.

Was that tension in the pulse flicking beneath his squared jaw? No, she'd imagined it. His body language spoke of easy confidence. And a bone-deep, almost indolent sex appeal that played havoc with her hormones.

'Nice to meet you, Alex.' She kept her voice blank. The fact he'd obviously towel-dried his black hair and not bothered to comb it, leaving it appealingly dishevelled, shouldn't make her itch to touch. As for the fact he was still barefoot, and hadn't buttoned his shirt, which showed a tanta-lising strip of taut skin...

'How are you boys feeling?' It was easier to con-centrate on them than this sudden rush of attrac-tion.

They murmured that they were okay, one even venturing a smile. They'd be fine, now the fright wore off. But she'd feel better when a professional checked them.

Alex stopped before her. 'Why don't you dry off while we take care of the boys and rustle up a warm drink? Downstairs, second cabin on the left. There's an en suite shower and I put out clean clothes you can wear till yours dry.'

Cat was about to refuse then thought better of it. George could put her ashore using the tender so she didn't have to swim back. She'd feel better knowing she didn't look like a drowned rat. Especially as her nipples were peaking insistently against her bra and she suspected her white T-shirt was transparent.

'Thanks. I will.' With a smile for George and the boys, she made her way downstairs.

The yacht was unlike any she'd seen. In her years as a bodyguard she'd been on massive, ultra-modern motor cruisers. Huge edifices several storeys high that housed not just a small boat, but a car and even a helipad. Those cruisers were built for socialising, for glamorous parties and sybaritic self-indulgence.

This yacht was nothing like that.

Cat passed through a wide cabin that was comfortable and stylish rather than *look-at-me* trendy, though no expense had been spared. Her hand slid down a polished teak rail as she followed the stairs into a roomy corridor. On either side were gleaming timber doors finished with brass touches. Everything was pristine yet the style belonged to an earlier, more gracious era.

She pushed open the second door and found an exquisite cabin, more wood on the walls, a deep plush carpet of dusk blue and a vast bed covered in crisp white and blue.

Wary of dripping onto the carpet, Cat moved quickly into the bathroom, where the luxury continued with marble and mirrors. It was hard to believe she was on a yacht, till she looked out the window and saw the sea and the shore bright in the early light.

Quickly she stripped and showered, tying back her hair with a band she found in the cupboard. There were clothes too. A brief black bikini and an oversized white shirt.

Cat frowned. But her shorts were sodden and she rejected the idea of putting on her wet T-shirt, knowing how it clung.

The bikini fitted surprisingly well and Cat felt a moment's annoyance that Alex had calculated her size then raided his private store of women's swimwear, no doubt kept especially for his lady friends.

Shoving her arms through the shirt sleeves, she rolled them up to her elbows, relieved at the way the oversized garment fell well down her thighs.

Cat hadn't missed the way Alex's eyes had gleamed as he surveyed her.

In other circumstances she might have been interested. But not now, not here, not while she was in St Galla on the most challenging job of her life.

Not while she was impersonating her royal sister.

Cat shivered and she hugged her arms around herself, rubbing away prickling gooseflesh and grateful for the soft fabric of the shirt she sincerely hoped was George's and not his boss's.

She'd had a bad feeling about this contract from the first. But it was only when she was installed in an exquisite guest apartment a corridor away from Princess Amelie's that Cat realised how completely she was out of her depth. They might share their father's royal blood but that was all.

No one would believe she was Amelie, not for a second.

Worse was the awful ache-in-the-belly certainty that it had been a mistake returning to the country where she'd been so desperately unhappy. Or to have anything to do with her distant family. She'd never belonged to them and they'd brought her nothing but trouble.

Buttoning the shirt as high as it would go, she

avoided the mirror and swivelled away, grabbing her sopping wet clothes.

She'd tell the Prime Minister she couldn't go through with it. He could have his deposit back. She hadn't spent a cent. He'd probably be grateful—the lady-in-waiting who'd been trying to tutor her in etiquette, deportment and the like had made it clear Cat wasn't fit for the role.

It would be a relief to get out of this place where even the scent of the sea and the pines crowding the rocky slopes evoked painful memories.

Cat emerged on deck with a determined step but pulled up when she found it deserted.

Everyone had gone, and so had the tender, she saw when she crossed to the rear of the vessel. The shower must have masked the sound of the motor.

'There you are.' That deep, smooth voice tantalised, trailing along her skin like a caress. 'Coffee or fresh juice?'

'Neither, thanks. It's time I left.' She glanced at her waterproof watch. It was still early.

Racked by doubts, she'd got little sleep and had gone running through the palace's private grounds as the first glimmers of dawn appeared.

She swung round and caught Alex's eyes on her bare legs.

Slowly, so slowly it must be deliberate, his gaze rose from her feet to her knees, then her thighs, lingering at the hem of the shirt before surveying her body so thoroughly she knew the shirt was transparent. By the time those blue eyes collided with hers, her arms were crossed over her breasts and her mouth was pursed.

'Do you do that to every woman?' Her chin hiked. She chose to ignore the little shiver of excitement that stirred in her belly at his obvious appreciation. For once the attraction was mutual.

He shook his head and Cat caught the curl of his mouth at one corner. 'Never. I'm making an exception with you.' His lips stretched into a full smile that did devastating things to her pulse. She should be furious at such a sexist attitude but strangely her anger was hard to hang on to. 'I'm returning the favour. You took your time looking at me.'

His stare defied her to argue and Cat clenched her jaw. She *had* got an eyeful of bare, some would say awesome, masculinity and she hadn't been eager to look away. She was in no position to object that he gave as got as he got.

Except that standing here in a brief bikini and see-through shirt, she felt vulnerable in a way she hadn't felt with any man.

Cat had spent a lifetime ensuring she was unassailable, emotionally and physically.

'Where are the others?'

'George is taking them to the recreation camp further up the coast. It turns out they took the canoe without permission and they started to think the staff might worry when they found it and them gone.'

'So how do I get ashore? Is there another boat?'

Alex shook his head. 'Just the tender. But George won't be long. In the meantime I'll get breakfast.'

'I really need to get ashore.'

'Well.' He tilted his head, appraising her. 'You could swim to the island. But you'd get wet all over again. Why don't you relax and let me cook for you?'

Cat turned, calculating the distance to the shore. She'd already run ten kilometres before shucking her shoes and diving in to help the boys. But she could swim back easily.

There was no reason to remain, not when she'd made up her mind to resign and turn her back on St Galla once and for all.

It hit her with a punch of disbelief that the only reason she hesitated was the man behind her.

She'd never known such instantaneous, full-on

attraction. The humour in those stunning eyes and his upfront attitude appealed as much as his hunky masculine body. Even the dark stubble shading that hard jaw made her want to touch him.

Cat had spent a lifetime learning how to keep guys at a distance, as colleagues or friends rather than lovers. This surge of awareness, the sudden feeling of connection was unique.

She turned back and found he'd moved closer, his bare footsteps silent. He was a mere arm's length away.

Cat hauled in a sharp breath. The combination of that half smile, the hint of citrus and warm male skin in her nostrils, and the certainty he felt the spark too, froze her to the spot.

It was there in the dilation of his pupils and the widening of his nostrils. He leaned towards her as if forced by the same compulsion for nearness. Yet he didn't touch.

The air vibrated as if an invisible cord tightened between them. Cat swallowed, her throat dry.

Abruptly he stepped back and the air emptied from her lungs in a whoosh.

'Breakfast? I do an excellent pancake.' His smile was easy, the intensity wiped from his expression. Yet his eyes were watchful. For all his overtly casual stance, he was alert, aware of every tiny tell-tale movement she made.

Like a predator scoping its prey.

It would be out of character but so easy for her to respond to his sexual pull. To laugh over breakfast and fall under the spell of that indigo gaze. For once in her life not to be prudent but to dive into what she knew instinctively would be a hot, steamy, thoroughly satisfying affair.

But it *was* out of character.

Plus she had enough on her mind with the need to escape the claustrophobic confines of the palace and the role she'd accepted. She wasn't cut out for deceit—masquerading as her half-sister and hiding her very personal reasons for wanting to visit the palace.

As much as her suddenly active hormones protested, Cat had to focus on setting things right.

'I'm sorry,' she said, not bothering to hide her regret. 'But I can't stay.'

She dropped her wet clothes and grabbed the hem of the shirt she wore, reefing it over her head then tossing it to Alex. He caught it one-handed against his chest.

His gaze didn't drop from her face but she *knew* he was aware of her every contour. She was aware of *him* from the soles of her feet to her peaking nipples and hammering pulse. And everywhere in between.

'I have to go.' Forcing herself to break his gaze, she turned, raised her arms and dived into the clear depths of the azure sea.

CHAPTER TWO

LEAVING ST GALLA wasn't as easy as Cat had hoped. How had she thought, after the lengths they'd gone to, and the money promised, they'd release her from her contract?

'Impossible.' The Prime Minister's voice over the phone was severe. 'I expect you to finish the job.'

'I'll return the first payment. Since arriving I've realised I can't pull this off. I'm a security professional, not an actor.'

'As a professional you'd know we wouldn't resort to this charade unless absolutely necessary. There's no other option.'

Silence hung between them.

'Princess Amelie isn't in danger, is she?' She'd asked before but got no answer.

The nation was still mourning the death in an accident of Amelie's younger brother, King Michel, and his wife. Cat had been stunned by the emptiness she'd felt after hearing the news, knowing she'd never have an opportunity to know her half-brother. Not that she'd anticipated *ever* meeting her half-siblings. Yet she'd followed the news with a fascinated dread, reading how, after the double funeral, Princess Amelie had cancelled her public appearances to spend time with her orphaned nephew, Sébastien.

Where were Amelie and the young Prince? Given the freedom Cat had to explore the beautiful Belle Époque palace and its grounds, they weren't here.

Cat regretted never knowing her brother. That sense of loss only strengthened her longing to meet her last living relatives: Amelie and Prince Sébastien.

'That need not concern you, Ms Dubois. Concentrate on the task for which you've been employed.' He paused. 'Remember the penalty clauses in your contract.'

Oh, she remembered. Massive financial penalties should she divulge the secret of what she was doing here. And for leaving before the requisite period was over.

But she hadn't yet begun the masquerade. 'Surely it's better to pull the plug now than when people realise we're trying to fool them? I've tried, but my tutor will tell you I'm a disaster in the role.' The woman made that clear with each sniff of her thin patrician nose.

'On the contrary, I've heard you're a quick study and you've made good progress.'

'Nevertheless—'

'Let me be clear, Ms Dubois.' Monsieur Barthe's voice was glacial. 'You will complete this assignment. If not, by the terms of the contract you have seven days to pay the penalty.'

Seven days to pay money she didn't have. The penalty payment was even larger than the total she'd earn.

'I trust you'll see the wisdom of staying.' He paused, but Cat couldn't think of a thing to say. 'Good. I'll see you at the reception.'

The phone went dead. Cat put it down, her stomach cramping. There was no way out. She shouldn't have agreed to take this on. Hadn't she known it from the first?

Never had the massive chasm between herself and the siblings she'd never known seemed wider. And her little nephew. Her heart had gone out to the tiny mite she'd seen on the news. His big, troubled eyes had tugged at her, but she was crazy to think she could help either of them.

Cat shook her head. She'd let sentiment and curiosity overcome sense.

Now she had to face the consequences.

She stared out the huge arched window of her

room. Beyond the manicured gardens, the pools and fountains and arbours, lay the wooded private royal reserve that encompassed the whole south-ernmost peninsula of the island nation. Beyond that was the sea.

Where Alex had his beautiful yacht.

For a second she let herself imagine she could simply walk out the door, swim to him and ask him to take her away. For she couldn't shake the bone-deep fear that in coming here she'd opened a door that should have remained firmly bolted. Like Pandora opening her box and releasing forces she'd never imagined.

Cat shivered, as if someone walked over her grave.

Nonsense. She didn't like it here because it re-minded her of the father who'd rejected her before she was born. And the shame she'd been made to carry through no fault of her own.

But she was strong and capable. She'd do the job, then leave without a backward glance. Simple.

Twenty-four hours later Cat walked carefully down the long ground-floor corridor, heels tapping on the beautiful parquetry floor. At her tutor's insis-tence she wore stockings, heels and a silk dress that swirled to her knees. Lady Enide had declared Cat would never convince anyone till she learned to walk in a dress.

Apparently she walked like a boy. Even if she did keep her shoulders back and her chin up.

Cat set her jaw and concentrated on balance. Teetering on stiletto heels was harder than *parcours*. Harder than karate. No wonder Lady Enide had left her to it, informing her crisply that they'd meet in forty minutes, by which time she expected to see Ms Dubois moving like a *lady*.

Cat's mouth curved in a mirthless smile. She'd always been a tomboy, rebelling against the inevitable comparisons between her and the graceful, ultra-feminine Princess who lived at the far end of their island nation.

It was easier for tomboys to pretend not to hurt when insults and innuendos rained down. And tomboys gave as good as they got when the insults became blows.

She didn't fancy her chances of convincing anyone she was an elegant lady.

Butterflies the size of kites twisted in her stomach. The Prime Minister had lied. Cat had just learned next week's event wasn't the simple affair he'd said.

Restlessly she pushed open a door and entered a grand reception room. It was white and gold, with ornate couches that looked as if they'd break if you sat on them. The mirrors were huge antiques, the chandeliers, she'd learned, brought from Versailles centuries ago. The paintings...she tried to recall which monarchs were in the paintings and failed.

Another black mark against her. She had to memorise everything about these rooms for the reception to celebrate five hundred years of amity between St Galla and distant Bengaria. It would be a glittering event.

And she'd been told minutes ago that the King of Bengaria would attend!

Her stomach cramped in horror. How did the Prime Minister expect her to fool a royal? It was madness. If she'd known she'd never have come. Which was no doubt why Monsieur Barthe hadn't broken the news earlier. He'd even tried to convince her their royal guest wouldn't see through her disguise since he'd never met Amelie!

As soon as she got a chance she'd look up the Bengarian King. For the first time her avoidance of all things royal worked against her. She shunned celebrity gossip about aristocratic families. She could so easily be fodder for those stories!

Cat shuddered. If she'd needed proof that this masquerade was desperately important for Amelie, this was it. Clearly Cat was covering for a crisis of some sort.

Maybe she could stand at the top of the elegantly curling staircase and wave her hand at the King without getting close? If she could keep her distance, and not talk, there was the slimmest chance she could bring off this charade.

Cat grimaced. From a distance no one would notice she was a smidgeon shorter than Amelie, her nose not quite as straight and her mouth a fraction wider. Or that she was smaller in the bust.

But to convince a king? Cat shook her head and pushed open the door to the next room.

On the threshold she stilled. Someone stood, silhouetted in the vast arched window.

A sensation, as if she rode a runaway roller coaster, plunged her stomach to the floor. Her hand clung to the door as she took in the tall figure, straight-shouldered, slim-hipped, long-legged.

Over his shoulder through the window a familiar yacht, streamlined, vintage and luxurious, lay anchored in the palace's private cove.

'You!' Cat's eyes rounded as he turned and that dark blue gaze snagged hers.

She'd told herself memory had exaggerated yesterday's sizzle of attraction. She'd been wrong. One look and sparks flashed under her skin, igniting heat deep within.

The instant of recognition stretched out and out.

Intriguingly, he now looked like an ad for some exclusive men's fashion house instead of a laid-back, sinfully sexy beachcomber. His dark hair was brushed back in a severe style that made her gaze linger on the sculpted perfection of his even, chiselled features. From head to toe he was suavely elegant, assured and breathtakingly male. Only the light dancing in those indigo eyes betrayed a hint of something else.

Despite her shock and instinctive caution, delight quivered through her as she read that look. He'd watched her that way yesterday. As if she were a delicacy he wanted to bite into.

'What are you doing here?' Her voice was stretched and too high as she stalked across the room, for once ignoring the sensation she was walking on stilts. 'How did you get in?'

'Through the front entrance. The butler asked me to wait here.' He smiled, a slow curl of the lips that fed a silly little shiver under her skin.

'I mean, *why* are you here?'

He lifted a hand, holding out a paper bag.

Hesitantly Cat took it and peered inside. Within lay her old running shorts. She recognised them from the frayed hem, and her ancient T-shirt, not only folded but ironed, if she wasn't mistaken. George had washed and ironed her gear. She couldn't imagine Alex doing anything so mundanely domestic.

Her gaze shot to his as she put the package down on the grand piano a few steps away.

'Thank you.' She paused, wondering how to handle this. 'That's very thoughtful.' Could she get rid of him quickly? She wasn't ready to play the part of Princess Amelie and admitting her real identity was impossible.

But how had he known where to find her? She'd said nothing about staying at the royal palace. She'd been running through the private royal reserve but assumed he'd think she'd trespassed, like the boys in the canoe who'd ventured into the palace's private zone.

Anxiety stirred. This scenario was wrong. There'd been no reason for Alex to look for her here.

'You don't look pleased to see me.' His voice was

easy, low enough to hum through her bones in a way that disturbed as much as it appealed.

Cat was no pushover when it came to men. It took more than a dark velvet voice and a hint of humour to win her over. Far more than a sexy, athletic body and stunning eyes. Yet there was something about Alex that broke through a lifetime's reserve. She didn't like it one bit.

'I'm...surprised.' She drew a quick breath. 'I didn't expect to see you again.' If circumstances had been different she'd definitely have wanted to pursue their acquaintance. But not like this.

If anyone discovered who she was the fallout would be disastrous.

Something about the lazy speculation in his eyes told her Alex saw far too much.

'I'm afraid the palace is closed to visitors at the moment.'

'So I gathered. The butler seemed surprised when I arrived.' Yet Alex made no move to leave. That speculative gaze was heavy as it took her in from head to toe.

Instinctively Cat drew herself up. She'd have to usher him out the door. 'I think it best if—'

'Why Cat?' He spoke at the same time.

'Sorry?'

'Your name. Is it a nickname because of your eyes?' When she didn't immediately answer he went on. 'I've never seen eyes quite that colour.'

'Cat's eyes?' She blinked. She'd never thought of that. People told her she had beautiful eyes but she'd never been convinced. Probably because through her early years they'd been the bane of her life. Such a distinctive colour, always commented on. Royal St Gallan it was called here because every member of the royal family for generations had inherited eyes that colour. Yet it was extraordinarily rare in the rest of the population.

When her mother had given birth to a girl only seven months after her hasty marriage to a man she'd never shown a preference for, and when that baby had eyes of Royal St Gallan green, there had been talk. People commented on how suddenly she'd left her job at the palace, and how it was whispered that the King had a roving eye despite his gorgeous wife and obviously happy family life.

'Cat?' He'd moved closer. The fresh scent of citrus and warm flesh invaded her nostrils. It sent tendrils of feminine pleasure curling through her.

She stiffened. This was *so* not good.

'It's what my friends call me.' That at least was true. She'd never been Catherine except to her stepfather, the man who'd treated her mother as a drudge and her as a disgusting burden despite the largesse he'd received for giving them his name.

'An unusual choice, but it suits.' His eyes crinkled at the corners as he smiled. Even in heels she was no match for his rangy height. Cat found herself wondering why she even noticed. She worked with guys all the time, some even taller than Alex.

'It was lovely of you to take so much trouble. Really.' Her muscles stretched taut as she forced a smile. 'But this isn't really a good time.' She stepped away, holding his gaze, inviting him to accompany her as she moved to the door.

'I understand.' Abruptly the hint of humour in his gaze disappeared. 'I should have begun by saying how very sorry I am. It must have been a tough time for you.'

'Sorry?' Cat frowned. From the moment she'd crossed the threshold nothing had made sense. Not seeing Alex here, looking urbane and remarkably at home, nor his interest in her name, nor the trouble he'd taken to return her ratty old running gear. And now he was sorry...?

'For your loss.' His mouth flattened and he raked a hand back through his hair, which immediately fell back into place. 'I'm not doing a very good job, am I? I should have offered my condolences when we met but you left so abruptly.'

The hair at Cat's nape rose as she read the sympathy in his eyes, the sincerity in the grim expression bracketing that generous mouth.

Anxiety stirred and doom-laden foreboding.

A large hand captured hers, long fingers enfolding it, warm and reassuring. 'You must be going through a hellish time, losing your brother and sister-in-law. You have my sympathy and my mother's. If there's anything I can do—'

He broke off when Cat stepped back, heart thundering, tugging her hand from his.

He thought she was Amelie.

The knowledge pressed down on her, stopping her breath, making her ears buzz and her head whirl as she stared up into that handsome, now sombre face.

Finally, hand to her sternum, she managed to gasp in air, sucking it deep and filling starved lungs.

Did he know Amelie? How well? How long before he realised Cat was an imposter?

And somewhere deep in her psyche, buried so deep she almost didn't register it, was a part of her that wanted to reach out and grab his hand again, feel that rush of heat and fortifying strength, because, absurdly, she *did* feel grief for the half-brother she'd never known and would now never know. Even though she had no right to feel anything.

She'd always been an outsider. These people weren't really her family, no matter the blood they shared.

'I...' She paused and forced a brittle smile. 'Thank you. That's very kind.' Her lips felt stiff and the words sounded stilted.

She wished she'd never got herself into this tangle of deceit. It went against everything she'd made of herself. Forced to hide her true identity since childhood, there'd been freedom and a welcome dignity and strength in building a life for herself that had no taint of subterfuge. Where she was simply Cat Dubois, capable, professional and open.

'I—' Cat broke off as the door opened behind her. Swinging round, she saw Lady Enide, immaculate as ever in a navy suit and pearls, her silver hair a testament to good taste and a personal stylist. The other woman paused on the threshold, her features morphing into a mask that even for her looked pinched and full of concern.

She stepped into the room and, to Cat's amazement, bent deep into a curtsey. The sort of curtsey she'd tried and failed to teach Cat.

'Your Highness. Welcome to St Galla.' Her eyes weren't on Cat but on Alex. Cat felt once more that enervating sensation as if her stomach had disconnected and plummeted at speed towards her toes.

'My apologies that you weren't greeted appropriately. The palace has only a skeleton staff during this period of mourning and we weren't expecting you yet.'

Colder and colder, Cat's spine froze vertebra by vertebra till it felt as if her backbone and neck were clamped in an icy vice.

Slowly she turned back to see Alex smiling. 'No need for apologies. As you can see, Princess Amelie has made me welcome.'

Eyes of rich blue met and held hers. She read curiosity and something that might have been satisfaction there. But she was too busy revisiting their conversation, wondering if she'd betrayed herself, to interpret his thoughts.

For the issue now wasn't merely her identity, and whether she could maintain a royal masquerade.

Worse was the fact Enide had called him 'Highness'. That the haughtiest, most proper woman she'd ever met had practically scraped the floor with her curtsey.

Which meant Alex wasn't merely a layabout yachtie.

Cat's brain galloped ahead to the guests expected for the St Gallan-Bengarian celebrations. Celebrations to commemorate an old alliance between the two nations, forged when St Galla fought annexation by both its mainland neighbours, France and Italy. Celebrations which the King of Bengaria would attend.

King Alexander.

Her breath stalled and for a horrifying moment she thought she'd crumple as her knees gave way.

Cat dropped her eyes from his bright, enquiring gaze and found herself staring at a pair of glossy hand-made shoes. She kept her eyes fixed on them, forcing down the surging rush of panic.

He was King Alexander of Bengaria.

And he believed her to be Amelie.

Could it get any worse?

Cat found herself sinking into a deep, perfectly executed curtsey. The sort of curtsey that had eluded her for days.

It was amazing what adrenaline and sheer panic could achieve.

'Welcome, Your Majesty. It's a pleasure to have you here.'

CHAPTER THREE

ALEX TWIRLED THE stem of his water glass, surveying his lunch companions. Lady Enide who, according to his mother, was warm-hearted despite
her frosty demeanour, kept the conversation rolling. They'd skated over the tragic deaths of King
Michel and Queen Irini to discuss Alex's mother's health, upcoming celebrations, trade talks, the
economy, the weather and even his yachting holiday.

His query about young Prince Sébastien, now
an orphan, was met with the news he was staying
with family friends away from prying eyes. The
news surprised Alex who'd assumed, like everyone else, that the boy was being cared for here by
his aunt. All reports indicated the two were close,
had been close even before the tragic accident that
killed the boy's parents.

Alex picked up tension in the room, camouflaged
by the polite small talk. Tension because he was

here, sooner than expected? Or because of something else?

The fact Princess Amelie... Cat clearly had no intention of mentioning they'd met already intrigued him. Why hide something so innocuous?

Unless the sudden blaze of attraction between them made her uncomfortable. *Something* did.

Beside Enide, Cat sat silently cutting her meal into ever smaller portions. It was only occasionally he managed to catch her eye.

What had happened to the confident, fascinating woman he'd met in the bay? She hadn't been daunted by an emergency situation or the sudden lightning strike of desire hammering the air between them. Instead of shrinking away, she'd returned his regard with clear interest.

Now, on the rare occasions their eyes met, she inevitably looked away first. She seemed in some way diminished, despite how beautiful she looked in a pale green silk dress that rustled provocatively when she moved.

Those soft sounds as she shifted interfered with his concentration. Alex kept remembering her sleek curves in the black bikini, tempting him through the light cover of his shirt.

'Do you swim often, Amelie?' He forced himself to use her proper name, sensing she wouldn't appreciate his use of her nickname here.

Her head jerked up and her eyes widened. Was that fear in those green depths? Again, she made it obvious she didn't want Enide to know they'd met. Fascinating.

At twenty-nine Amelie was a capable woman, soon to be proclaimed Regent for Prince Sébastien till he came of age. Surely there was no reason to hide their unconventional meeting.

'I enjoy swimming but I don't get a lot of time for it.'

'Perhaps while I'm here you could show me your favourite swimming place.'

She paused and Enide answered first. 'The cove immediately below the palace has always been the royal family's favourite.' She turned to the younger woman and Alex read a hint of stiffness. 'Hasn't it, Amelie?'

Amelie nodded. 'Yes, it's beautiful there.'

What it was about the exchange that put him on alert, Alex didn't know. Yet he knew something was wrong. There was a constraint about Cat... Amelie that hadn't been there before.

'And I see you have an extra-large swimming pool. Which do you prefer, the sea or the pool?'

He was talking idly, trying to fathom what was going on.

Did he imagine Cat's flickering gaze towards their chaperone? For it had become clear Lady Enide was just that—keeping a watchful eye on them. Alex didn't know whether to be amused or annoyed.

Did the St Gallans think because they'd suggested a royal marriage, he'd take that as carte blanche to scoop Cat up and into his bed before the banns were read? He wasn't that medieval.

Yet the idea was ridiculously tempting.

Despite not wanting a wife.

'I usually do laps, but there's a freedom about swimming in the sea, don't you think?' This time when her gaze met his there was the hint of a smile and response tugged deep in his belly. Whatever this was between them: lust, fascination, the temptation to cut loose after three long years with his nose to the grindstone, it fired his libido like flame to pure alcohol.

'I couldn't agree more. There's nothing more invigorating than an early morning dip in the sea.'

Was it imagination or did something ignite in that clear gaze? Did she too remember how it had been between them—he naked and she as good as with her sopping clothes—as arousal roared into life?

Alex wanted that again. Wanted it more than he'd wanted anything for years.

Because he'd denied himself so many things since inheriting the throne? Because his responsibilities didn't leave time for anything as selfish as uncomplicated sex with a beautiful woman?

Or because there'd been something about Cat that he'd connected with instantly?

How long since he'd bantered with a woman, flirted and enjoyed that frisson of sexual desire? He'd been too busy delving into the murky morass of his father's financial affairs, the contracts given to friends and those offering backhanders. His father had run the country as if it were his personal piggy bank to be plundered. Alex had spent three years turning the tide, avoiding national bankruptcy by the skin of his teeth and slowly clawing back control of the national finances from his father's grasping cronies.

Now, on vacation for the first time in years, he was ready for a little dalliance. The problem was he'd set his sights on the woman his mother and all his advisers had pegged for his wife.

No way would he make a move on Cat... Amelie. Not when it would be construed as a statement of marital intent.

An affair, on the other hand…

A mutually enjoyable short-term affair for the length of his stay…

Lust corkscrewed through his belly as their eyes met and that high-octane blast of awareness reverberated.

'Perhaps we could swim together tomorrow?' he suggested.

Cat opened her mouth but Lady Enide spoke swiftly, her tone cool. 'Unfortunately the Princess will be busy tomorrow.' Alex stared and, seeing his surprise, Enide hurried on. 'It's regrettable, Your Majesty. Unfortunately we weren't expecting you quite so soon.'

There was more to it than that. But what? There was something more than officious about the way the older woman hovered over Cat. It reminded him of the anxious way his mother had watched his father when he was in one of his moods. As if preparing to deal with his freak tempers.

More and more intriguing.

Cat seemed anything but highly strung. She'd impressed with her calm competence in the water, her self-assurance and capability. Today, though subdued, she'd given no signs of the self-absorption and unsteady ego that had characterised his father.

'Another day, then. I'm here for some time.' Alex leaned back, watching the ripple of consternation on Enide's face.

He sensed a mystery.

'You're not travelling on and then returning for the festivities?' Cat spoke, her voice calm yet with a telling husky edge that sharpened his libido. Surprising how arousing it was to sit across a formal dining table from a woman dressed in silk and heels and imagine her in his bed, naked and eager.

Even the dragon guarding her was a challenge rather than a real obstruction. Alex might be out of practice, but he'd always been successful with women, even before it looked as if he might inherit a throne.

He just needed to discover if Cat felt the same undertow of desire.

'I'm afraid any plans to sail on to Italy have been put on hold. The yacht has to go into dry dock for repair.'

George would be surprised, but Alex sensed dragon lady's unwillingness to have him in the palace and he was determined to find out why.

And give her no chance to deny him. The fact she was so obviously on edge at having their guest of honour arrive early set him on alert. Besides, George *had* talked about the need for work on the yacht one day.

'In that case you must stay here.' Lady Enide's mouth curved in a smile as welcoming as hoar-frost.

Beside her, Cat swallowed. Did he imagine it or did her pupils widen?

'Amelie?' Despite his burning curiosity he wouldn't thrust himself into her home, especially after her recent loss, if *she* objected.

'I'm sure you'll be more comfortable here than in the city. There's plenty of room, after all.' Her jaw angled infinitesimally higher, banishing the earlier hint of reserve. 'I'll ask the chef to make pancakes for breakfast while you're here.'

A hint of a smile softened her mouth and under-standing passed between them, the memory of him offering to cook her pancakes on the yacht.

'Pancakes?' Lady Enide looked perplexed.

'I heard somewhere that His Highness is fond of pancakes.'

'Alex, please.' He relaxed back in his seat, pleased Cat was taking the lead. Her silence had puzzled him. 'Yes, I'm fond of pancakes. I acquired a taste for them when I worked in the States.'

It wasn't till the next day that he managed time alone with her. Time enough to wonder if he'd acted too rashly, inviting himself to the palace he'd originally planned to visit for only the shortest of official visits.

Yet it was too late for second thoughts.

He'd been installed in a guest suite with views on two sides to the manicured gardens and the sea beyond. He had everything he could wish for, except the company of his hostess.

It was only a couple of months since Cat had lost her brother. She had other priorities. Yet he was disappointed when a staff member showed him the palace. And when Lady Enide, with a posse of senior diplomats and the Prime Minister, met him for afternoon tea in one of the grand rooms. There was no sign of Cat, merely a murmured reference to a previous commitment she couldn't break.

At dinner they sat with the full length of the long table between them. Afterwards his attempt to talk with her was stymied by the Prime Minister, inviting him to discuss trade opportunities Alex couldn't afford to ignore.

Strange behaviour for a woman who'd consented to the idea of marriage, should he agree. It felt, bizarrely, as if she didn't want to be alone with him.

Now, so early that dew clung to the grass and the sun's rays sprayed apricot and amber across the sea, he intercepted Cat on her morning run. He'd woken early and dressed in jogging gear. He'd seen her don running shoes after swimming ashore from the yacht and guessed she was an early morning runner. Now he peeled away from his vantage point and joined her.

Startled, she looked over her shoulder. Her expression was unreadable as she nodded acknowledgement. Yet she didn't break stride as she headed for a path descending into the forest reserve.

Alex followed, adapting to her pace. It wasn't a jog but a long-legged run, quickly eating up the distance. He found himself needing to concentrate on his breathing even as he enjoyed the flash of her smooth golden legs and the sway of that long ponytail over her slim back.

She moved like an athlete, not a royal who spent her days glad-handing VIPs and hosting formal dinners.

Princess Amelie was a poster girl for modern royalty. Losing her mother early, she'd become her father's official hostess, the pretty face of royalty in St Galla, often filling in for the King at openings, community events and charity occasions. She was a consummate diplomatic hostess and the media loved her for her warm heart and cool elegance, citing her as a modern-day Princess Grace.

Word had it she'd virtually raised her younger brother, Michel, and that she had a special fondness for children. It was this maternal side of her nature that had particularly appealed to his mother. As if he was ready to settle down with a brood of kids!

It wasn't Cat's assets as a mother that focused his attention as they ran the waterfront path through the forest. It was imagining that supple golden body wrapped around him, those soft lips on his, and that voice, throaty with desire, murmuring his name.

Even her hair made him want to tangle his fingers to draw her close. It pleased and intrigued him that it fell in abundant golden waves, so different to the photos he'd seen and the way she'd looked last night, hair tight and straight in a formal style. There was a hint of wildness about it now that suited her. Like the flash and sizzle he'd read in her the day they'd met.

Each time he saw her Alex was struck by how different the Princess was in the flesh, compared with her photos. In those she always looked refined and charming. But the real woman also had a vitality and undeniable sex appeal that drew him.

Drew him! It was a smack to his chest, stealing his air.

'You run well.' She'd stopped, hands on knees, drawing slow breaths, though he noticed she wasn't panting. Her T-shirt clung to her breasts and abruptly he was aware not only of the trickle of sweat down his backbone but the heat stirring in his belly that had nothing to do with exertion.

Hands on hips, he hauled in oxygen, chest expanding hungrily. How long since he'd had a good run instead of a snatched gym workout after a long day?

Cat's eyes dropped to his chest then roved up to his shoulders before cutting away to the glassy sea.

'So do you.' Alex tried and failed to divert his attention from her pert breasts and the pulse beating at the base of her neck where her skin glowed, damp and inviting.

Okay, maybe he didn't try very hard.

He lifted his eyes and met her clear gaze.

His lungs constricted. What he read there was unequivocal. Interest. Attraction. Desire.

She didn't hide it coyly. There were no slanting sidelong looks or fluttering eyelashes, just an appraisal that seared through his self-control and made him want to punch the air in victory.

So he hadn't imagined it. Despite the distance she'd put between them yesterday, Cat's direct gaze spoke of a need that answered his own.

A breeze stirred loose tendrils of her hair and he'd swear he tasted her fragrance on his tongue. Something crisp and sweet like ripe pears.

She swallowed, the tip of her tongue swiping her bottom lip, and his mouth dried.

He forced himself to keep his hands anchored at his waist, fingers digging into taut flesh.

Cat blinked and stepped away, turning to look across the bay where his yacht had been moored yesterday. She wrapped her arms around herself.

'When did you recognise me? You never called me Amelie that first day.'

'On the yacht.' Not as soon as he should have. He'd been too distracted by the urgent hum of hunger. A hunger so sudden and complete it outclassed anything he'd ever felt for a woman. If it weren't for the fact he was coming out of a prolonged sexual drought it would worry him. Fortunately he knew this must be his libido's response to recent abstinence and a remarkably intriguing woman.

'You didn't say anything.' Was it imagination or did her mouth tighten?

He shrugged. 'Was there any need? It was clear we were going to get to know each other.' He hadn't intended it, but his voice hit a gravel-deep level at the thought of how well he'd like to know her. 'You're easily recognisable, even in wet clothes.'

The clinging clothes had merely turned the picture-perfect Princess into a real flesh-and-blood woman, much more appealing than in any of those posed photos. There was an aura about Cat, a vibrant authenticity, that drew him. He felt it now, when at last night's dinner it had been subdued.

'Cat... Amelie.'

She swung to face him, her expression grave. 'Yes?'

Alex cleared his throat. Absurd to hesitate. He needed to clarify his position, even if it scuppered the chance to know Cat as he wanted to. He refused to lead her on. He could forgive most things but he abhorred falseness. Growing up with his conniving, deceitful father, Alex was upfront in all his dealings and expected that from others.

'I need to clear something up.'

'Yes?' She squared her shoulders, her chin tipping as if waiting for a blow.

'About the marriage proposal.'

She blinked, her pupils widening as if they might engulf her eyes.

Alex hesitated. Could she really have invested so much in the idea of a match between them? She struck him as down-to-earth, not the sort of female who'd languish waiting for her advisers to arrange a dynastic match.

But how well did he know her beyond the sexual attraction saturating the air between them?

'The marriage proposal?' Again that quick swipe of her bottom lip. Alex's belly curled in on itself, heat quickening.

'I know your advisers thought a match between us was desirable. I know you thought so too or it would never have been raised with my staff.'

Her features froze into blankness and he paused. He didn't want to make it sound like he was rejecting *her*. Far from it. It was the idea of marriage he wasn't ready for.

'There *are* advantages.' He paused and hated his hesitation. 'But the truth is I'm not interested in marriage. Not yet.'

She said nothing. Her expression was unreadable. Only the flickering pulse at her throat and the rise and fall of her breasts under the thin cotton proved she hadn't frozen in place.

Because she was insulted? Disappointed? Despite his scrutiny he could read nothing in her body language.

'You don't want to marry,' she said at last. Her voice held an off-key note he couldn't place. Not disappointment or hurt, but *something*.

He nodded. 'I thought you needed to know straight away.'

Cat nodded, her head jerking as if pulled by some unseen puppeteer. It was all she could do to keep her features blank as she hid horror.

What had she walked into?

What had they deliberately dropped her into?

The Prime Minister had said she'd only need to appear at one small official function. It was only after arriving that she'd discovered King Alex of Bengaria would also be at the reception. Now he'd arrived early, before she was anywhere near ready to play the role, and she discovered there were plans for an engagement. Had Monsieur Barthe planned to break that to her too?

She locked her knees as they wobbled and her heart somersaulted crazily against her ribs.

How could anyone expect her to fool the man who was going to marry Amelie?

Or, it seemed, who wasn't going to marry her after all.

Cat's emotions were an unholy tangle as she met that intense blue stare. There was dismay and, yes, fright, at how easily she might have betrayed her identity.

Plus…was it relief that Alex wasn't planning to marry her half-sister?

Guilt twisted her insides.

Sternly Cat told herself this was none of her business, except to the extent he never realised her true identity. Behind the easy attitude she sensed a core of steel, and pride. No man, especially one like that, would want a stranger listening to words meant for his fiancée, or almost fiancée.

Were they actually engaged? Or hadn't arrangements got that far?

A sudden sick feeling in her stomach made her step away and prop herself one-handed against a tree, inhaling the sharp scent of pine needles and saltwater. Rough bark bit her palm and she focused on that, rather than the rush of confusion and fear.

'Cat?' Concern edged his deep tone, feathering her skin in a wash of goosebumps. 'Are you okay?'

'Of course.' She hauled in sustaining oxygen and raised her gaze. He stood close. Too close. His brow crinkled. There was regret in his expression.

'I didn't mean to hurt you.'

She straightened, chin rising. 'You didn't.' Except, strangely, that's how it felt. As if he'd rejected *her*.

It didn't matter that she wasn't who he thought. Or that never in her wildest dreams would she fantasise about marrying someone like Alex. Her illegitimacy was a stain that had destroyed her mother's life and made Cat's early years hell. Pure bloodlines were paramount to the aristocracy. She'd never fit into that world and didn't want to.

'Apart from anything else, I'm not a fan of arranged marriages.' He paused and she read tension in his face. 'It's not common knowledge but I know I can trust you. My parents' marriage was an utter disaster. They didn't know each other before the wedding and then had a lifetime to regret their mistakes.'

His broad shoulders lifted and fell. 'It didn't matter to my father since he only wanted my mother's money and a suitable hostess. My mother suffered but felt obliged to stick it out, especially after I was born.' His mouth twisted. 'I'd never marry a woman I barely knew. It wouldn't be fair to either of us.'

Cat stared, torn between shock at his revelation and a gush of emotion, hot and heady, as she realised how much she liked his honesty and attitude.

'So, where do we go from here?' She was wary of saying too much, afraid to mention an engagement if there wasn't one.

He shrugged. 'Nowhere. I'll simply have my people tell your people that we won't proceed.' He ducked his head a fraction as if trying to read her expression. But Cat had donned her professionally impervious look. The one that deflected the most aggressive intrusion. She'd had plenty of practice. Stonewalling prurient curiosity was a tactic she'd learned in childhood.

'Cat? Say something.'

'What do you want me to say? It seems pretty straightforward from where I'm standing.'

But what about Amelie? Was she in love with Alex? Did she have her heart set on marriage? Surely that was impossible. Yesterday had confirmed Amelie and Alex had never met. Their countries lay half a continent apart and Alex hadn't expected to inherit the throne till recently. There'd been no connection between them.

Which made her wonder anew what her half-sister was like. Why agree to marry a stranger as if she were a piece of merchandise on approval before purchase?

Cat couldn't imagine any circumstances where she'd agree to such a cold-blooded arrangement.

But she hadn't been raised royal, had she?

'You're okay with this?'

She opened her mouth to say it wouldn't matter if she wasn't. He'd made up his mind and that was the end of it. But she thought better of it. Truly, she didn't know what to say. Any mistake could unmask her.

'Cat?' A large hand cupped her cheek and tilted her face till she lost herself in eyes the colour of a twilight sky. She dragged in a sharp breath alive with the aroma of citrus and hot male skin. It was a heady combination. Too heady. She made to step back but instead came up against the trunk of a pine tree.

'I mean what I say. This isn't about you; it's about me. I'm not up for marriage yet, despite what my mother thinks.'

'Your mother?' Cat swallowed hard, trying to

ignore the heat of his hand and the detonations of pleasure where his hand touched her flesh. She'd never known anything like this instant, consuming response to a man. It distracted her when she needed focus.

He smiled, his taut features softening in a way that made her pulse quicken and her hormones wake. With his black hair flopping over his brow and that smile tugging his lips he was too charismatic. Handsome as Prince Charming but with a lethal edge of sex appeal more raw and real than any make-believe hero.

'Strange, isn't it, that after her experience she's trying to arrange a marriage for me? She always said your mother was a sweetheart, one of the nicest, kindest women she'd known. She was convinced her daughter would make a perfect wife, even without the political advantages of a match. That's why she proposed the idea.' He shrugged. 'Of course the fact St Galla's treasury could put Bengaria back in the black isn't to be sneezed at.'

So what would Amelie have got from the deal? Marriage to Alex. That's what.

With his hand still cupping her face, his eyes twinkling and his long, lean body hemming her in, Cat felt a ripple of longing. Not for a royal marriage but for this man who awoke desires she'd sublimated too long.

Move away. Break his hold. Say something.

The orders from her brain came loud and clear but Cat found herself simply holding his gaze, listening to the unsettled thrum of her pulse and watching the amusement in his eyes die.

His touch tightened and need quivered through her.

It should be impossible. He was a stranger. A danger to her job here, a man she knew next to nothing about.

Yet what she felt was real and strong. Pure and true as the swell of the sea on the pristine beach nearby.

'Tell me you understand.' His breath warmed her lips. His thumb stroked back and forth across her cheek.

Cat nodded. 'You don't want to marry.'

'I've got too much to do. There's still so much work to get Bengaria back on track. I haven't got time for a wife. I'm not ready to be a father.'

Yet Alex didn't draw back. If anything, he seemed closer.

'If I wanted a bride it would be different.' His voice was husky.

Cat didn't trust herself to speak. His expression held her spellbound, though logic screamed that she needed to put distance between them.

'If I wanted a bride I couldn't go past those big green eyes. Or those lips. I'd be suggesting we got to know each other *much* better.' His thumb dipped from her cheek to her mouth, pressing her lower lip and dragging it down. Cat exhaled, lungs tight, nipples budding against the constraint of her bra as his thumb stroked her lip, once, twice, till she couldn't resist and tasted him with the tip of her tongue. He was salt and spice and frighteningly addictive.

His eyes dilated, his breath warm on her face, he crowded closer, long legs bracketing hers. His other arm stretched out to the tree trunk behind her as if Alex too felt the sudden need for safe anchor as the ground seemed to ripple and swell.

'And as for this body...' To her dismay his hand dropped but before she could frame a protest she felt his touch, tantalising and soft, brush her collarbone then trace the wide neckline of her T-shirt, before sliding down.

Cat's breath stalled as his knuckles brushed the outer swell of her breast, slowing then tracing down her ribs then splaying at her waist. Those long, hard fingers made her aware of how small she was compared with him. Of how much strength resided in those large capable hands and that taut athletic body.

Her mouth was parched but she had to find words to make him back off. This was too dangerous. To her masquerade but also to *her*. She teetered on the brink of feelings that made a mockery of all her training, her strength and control. She swallowed and moistened her lips with her tongue then opened her mouth to speak.

But the words didn't come because Alex's mouth settled on hers and the world exploded.

CHAPTER FOUR

A SHUDDER OF satisfaction ripped through him as he delved into Cat's mouth. The hairs on his nape lifted and his flesh prickled in a wash of excitement.

Yes.

, *This.*

He angled his head for better access and found his eyes closing as he concentrated on the lush, moist warmth of her. Cat tasted like no other woman. A flavour he couldn't name, yet had surely craved all his life.

He let go of the tree and cupped her jaw, caressing, holding her still when she would have moved. A mighty shudder racked her. He heard the swift intake of her breath and knew she felt that slam of recognition too.

Instinctively he crowded her against the pine tree, not hard, but enough to stymie an easy escape. He needed her here, where he could explore the *rightness* of them together.

It must be an illusion. Yet it felt as if their bodies recognised and welcomed each other.

But he'd never met Cat till two days ago. Neither at an official function or even incognito in the years he'd worked as a pilot. He'd have remembered her taste, those stunning eyes, and the vibrant challenge of her.

He'd swear he'd be able to identify this woman even if he were blindfolded.

She refused to kiss him back, standing rigid. But he'd heard the hum of pleasure she hadn't been able to stifle, felt that initial tremor of delight. He loosened his grip on her waist and dragged his fingers up over her ribcage and a shudder ripped through her.

Alex stifled a smile of satisfaction.

He should resist this as she tried to. Getting tangled up with Princess Amelie at the same time as rejecting an offer to marry her was fraught with potential disaster.

Yet the tug of need was so compelling he couldn't shut it off.

Didn't want to shut it off.

This was about sex, not dynastic machinations. It was raw and real, not finessed.

After years of royal duty this was a lungful of

clean air after claustrophobia. Like putting a new jet through its paces, the freedom of skimming to the horizon on a slipstream of pure adrenaline.

He slid his hand from her jaw, across that smooth cheek to her thick, silky hair. Desire spiked, driving heat through his belly as he dug his fingers in, revelling in that rich softness and enjoying her tell-tale movement as she tilted her head into his caressing hand.

Deftly he pulled away the tie that kept her hair up and again she moved, helping him. Then his hands were cupping her skull as he deepened the kiss.

Her hands rose to his arms. He felt her tight grasp as if she'd wrench his hands away. Her chest expanded mightily, pushing those ripe breasts against his torso and sending his blood south in a sudden rush.

Tension held him immobile, knowing and hating she was about to break away when he wasn't ready to stop.

But she surprised him. Her hands slid up his shoulders, clinging tight and strong, tugging him closer, not pushing away.

With a soft sound that might have been relief or possibly dismay, she leaned in. Her breasts crushed against him, her lithe body supple and urgent in all the right places.

Then she was kissing him back with an urgency that sent the last of his control spiralling into nothingness.

She was flame and silk and cushioned invitation against him. Her ardour matched his as she kissed him back like she wanted to fuse to him.

Cat welcomed his tongue into her mouth, melting against him. Her kiss was so sensuous, so eager, it knotted him with sexual hunger. Her barely-there sigh of delight, almost drowned out by the rough punch of his pulse, made him crazy.

Sex was fun, satisfying and sometimes urgent. It was never out of control. Never like this.

Whatever this was with Cat, he refused to give it up. Not yet.

Cat had never felt like this. As if a volcano of need exploded inside her, disintegrating every boundary, every thought.

Mouth welded to Alex's, she felt pure desire, urgent, mind-blowing.

She tried to pull back, to stop. But how could you stop a force of nature? It was cataclysmic yet wonderful. Sinfully dangerous yet searingly pure and real. Impossible to resist, though she'd done her best.

For this instant there was no gulf between them, no difference in social strata, no hidden identity, no lies. Nothing but bliss and a driving urgency to take this man as hers. An urgency she'd never known with anyone. It was utterly foreign to her cautious nature and the control she always strove for.

Was that why it felt like heaven to lose herself so completely in his arms? Because it was letting go as she'd never allowed herself to do?

She pushed against him, imprinting the rich, intense flavour of him on her sense memory. Everything about him, from his size to his hard masculine muscle and the slight prickle of his unshaved jaw, incited her to a level of sexual recklessness that was utterly unfamiliar.

Her knees turned liquid and she dimly realised it was only his body and the tree behind her that kept her upright. Yet instead of a warning siren in her head all she registered was that she wanted more. She wanted—

Alex's hands dropped to her shoulders and, before she knew what he was about, he'd pulled back, holding her where she was so that a waft of sultry sea air drifted between them.

Her eyes snapped open and she lost herself in his cobalt stare. Did she imagine a kick of adrenaline as their gazes met and held? He looked ridiculously handsome, like a fantasy made flesh, yet his hard grip on her shoulders and his hot breath on her face were real. As was the desperate, clawing need to have him kiss her again.

Cat drew a shaky breath, then another, telling herself sanity would return if only she could break away.

But the dreadful truth was that she didn't want to get away.

Alex leaned in, lowering his forehead to hers. One hand cupped her cheek, his thumb stroking back and forth as if driven by the same restlessness that coiled within her.

'Cat.' Just that. But that deep voice whispering her name sounded like a benediction.

She shivered and lifted her hand to his jaw, exulting in the scrape of bristles across her palm. Excitement juddered through her, tightening her nipples and making her press her thighs together. Never, even working in the male-dominated world of personal protection, had she been as deliciously, exultantly conscious of the tantalising differences between male and female.

'We can't do this.' She hadn't been aware of the words forming and almost didn't recognise that husky whisper as hers.

She sucked in a breath that tasted of him. For a dizzying second she was afraid she'd tilt her head up to his, begging for another kiss. But she needn't have feared. A second later he was gone, moving out of reach. She slumped against the rough-barked tree. Cat clamped her teeth against her instinctive protest.

Alex stood, apparently watching the wind ruffle the pearlescent sea. Only the ticking of the pulse in his jaw and the deep rise of his chest as he dragged in air hinted that he too felt the effects of their kiss.

Determined, Cat tried to shut her mind to that. It was too subversively enticing. Yet she couldn't stop eating him with her eyes, from the solid plane of his jaw to the strong line of his aristocratic nose. From the width of his shoulders to the heavy muscle of his powerful thighs.

'There's a solution.' He raked his hand back through hair the colour of midnight and Cat felt a squiggle of delight that she, Cat Dubois, was the one who had him on edge. It was stupid. Any connection between them must be disastrous, but it would have been intolerable if she'd been the only one experiencing this.

'There can't be.' She pushed herself off the tree. She needed to put more distance between them. But she couldn't get her feet to move.

He swung around and there it was again, a zap of energy arcing between them as real as if he'd reached out and caressed her.

Cat swallowed and worked on making her face unreadable. She had to stop this madness.

'Forget our positions for a moment.' His voice was low, coaxing. 'Forget the idea of a royal marriage.' He paused, his gaze drifting over her before returning to hold hers. 'You deserve more than an arranged marriage anyway. You've got such passion, Cat. A woman like you deserves to marry a man who loves her, not some bridegroom chosen for his pedigree.'

Cat bit down a mirthless laugh at the idea of anyone arranging a marriage for her. As for the question of pedigree…hers was irredeemably tainted by illegitimacy.

Alex couldn't have said anything that highlighted more starkly the gulf between them—he a blue-blooded noble with all the benefits of a privileged

upbringing and first class education and she... She
shook her head, her hair brushing her cheeks, reminding her of his hands there, moulding, caressing.

'You said there's a solution.' Anything to resolve
this diabolical situation would be a godsend. She'd
realised she was in over her head pretending to be
Amelie even before Alex arrived. But now...she
didn't have a clue how to go on.

'It's simple.' His smile was slow and bone-melting. 'We have an affair.'

'Sorry?' Had her hearing been affected as well
as her body and her brain?

'You heard me.' He shifted his weight as if about
to close the gap between them then apparently
thought better of it and rocked back on his heels.
'There's no reason we can't be lovers. I'll be gone
next week, as soon as the festivities are over, and
I won't return. It's unlikely we'll see each other
again, except maybe in the distant future as guests
at someone else's royal wedding or coronation. In
the meantime, why not enjoy ourselves?'

Cat gaped up at him. Enjoy themselves? As simple as that? As if scandal and subterfuge didn't
surround them on all sides?

It wasn't just the threat of discovery and disaster

that worried her. There was the fact that her initial, overwhelming response was eagerness. She wanted to lie in this man's arms, feel him possess her, take him inside her and feel him come apart. She wanted to orgasm from his touch and drown in the dark blue depths of his eyes.

She wanted him so profoundly, she knew instinctively it was perilous. Her most important life lesson had been to trust in no one, rely only on herself. Isolation had shaped her from the day she could understand the condemning whispers about her mother and the resentment in her stepfather's eyes.

With Alex she was in danger of wanting too much.

Yet she barely knew him! How much more would she want if they became lovers? She feared this man could make her dream of things she could never have, and should never want.

'No!' She straightened, moving away to look across the sea, searching for calm. 'It's not possible.'

'Of course it's possible. Given the way we were a couple of minutes ago, it's a miracle we're not busy making it a reality right now, here on a bed of pine needles.'

Cat's head whipped around at the raw note in his usually smooth voice. Their gazes met and clung and suddenly, shockingly, she could see it clearly—the pair of them, naked, straining together in the peachy early morning light. His long, strong form blanketing hers, his hands running restlessly over her, hauling her ankles up over his hips as he plunged deep with a single, sure thrust.

Fire spread in her veins. She felt it crimson her throat and cheeks and knew he read its significance. His gaze darkened as if he shared the same erotic image.

Cat snapped her gaze back to the brilliance of the sun on the sea. 'I wouldn't have let it get that far.'

He didn't reply. He didn't need to. They both knew he, not she, had been the one to pull back.

'Just because there's…attraction.' She paused, wondering if any word could adequately describe the primitive need that had roared to life within her. 'That doesn't mean we have to follow through. We'll go our separate ways after next week's celebration.'

If she ever made it that far. Cat couldn't imagine maintaining this charade for another hour, much less a week.

'That's exactly why we should become lovers.'

Alex's voice slowed and deepened on the last word, as if he savoured it. Prickles of awareness rippled across her skin. 'We both want that. You can't deny it. Lovers for a week with no strings attached—it's the perfect solution.'

'Do you always give in to temptation?' She tried to dredge up anger at his casual attitude, remind herself how disciplined she'd had to be to achieve what she had—independence from St Galla and a successful career. But it did no good because, despite a lifetime's training in self-denial and focus, she craved the same thing he did—relief from the most potent sexual craving she'd ever experienced.

His eyes bored into hers. 'You of all people must know I don't. I spend all my time doing my duty. I spend days locked in meetings and too much time at gala functions and official ceremonies. I suspect not even our advisers truly know what it means to be responsible for a kingdom and carry that burden under the full glare of public attention. That's something we have in common.'

Alex rolled his shoulders and for the first time Cat saw a hint of weariness in the grooves beside his firm mouth. Devastatingly, that only made him more, not less appealing.

He laughed but there was no humour in the

sound. 'I never expected to be King, you know, even though my father was Regent for years. My cousin Stefan should be on the throne.' He frowned and she glimpsed a serious man behind the devastating charisma and charm. Cat leaned closer, responding to the sadness she heard behind his clipped words.

'Unfortunately Stefan died suddenly and my father became King.' Something about the way he spoke made her wonder what his father had been like. There was none of the affection she'd heard when he spoke of his cousin.

'When *he* died I had to give up the career I loved to return to Bengaria and the throne. It's been a steep learning curve.'

After a couple of days trying to walk in Amelie's shoes, literally, Cat was in awe of anyone coming in cold to a royal role and making a success of it. And she'd been learning the easy stuff, not how to lead a country.

Admiration stirred, making Cat tense. If only she'd learn something about him she *didn't* like.

'You want me to feel sorry for you?' She planted her hands on her hips. Yes, he'd had to give up his career but there were far worse things in the world.

Like always being an outsider. Never belonging. Even in her chosen profession Cat lived and worked on the fringes of other people's lives, keeping them secure. Alex had privilege, a real family. He belonged.

'Would sympathy make you sleep with me?' A flashing grin tore at the indignation she strove to shore up. She discovered she was no more immune to the devilry she read there than she was to the shimmering invitation in his eyes. She rubbed her hands up and down her bare arms as a crop of goosebumps covered her flesh.

'Of course not.' She tried to sound dismissive but the effect was more grumpy than superior. Like a woman forced to deny herself what she most wanted.

The trouble was that, despite every logical argument, Alex's outrageous proposition was too tempting.

'The morning we met was my first day off in three years.' Alex's expression sobered. 'I'd planned to sail on to Italy for a short vacation before returning for the festivities. I didn't intend to visit the palace till later.' His jaw tightened and Cat saw his hands clench. 'But then I met you.'

Cat frowned, filling in the silence that followed

his words, not quite believing what it meant. 'You said your yacht—'

He lifted those powerful shoulders. 'It's getting some maintenance work. But it wasn't urgent.' He paused and Cat's blood pounded in her ears.

'The only reason I stayed was you.' His mobile lips quirked up at one side and something tumbled over inside her. 'I met you and had to see you again.'

Denial clawed its way up Cat's constricting throat. He couldn't mean that. It was preposterous. The sort of over the top compliment given by a sexy man intent on seduction.

Yet the Internet search she'd done last night indicated that, despite his charm and humour, King Alex of Bengaria wasn't a flagrant womaniser. He worked hard and was generally credited with turning around his country's ailing prospects. The only photos of him with girlfriends were ones taken before he'd become King. Cat had learned he liked slim brunettes and, to her disgust, had felt jealous when she saw him with one after another glamorous, ultra-feminine beauty glued to his side.

Cat's hair swung round her cheeks as she shook her head. 'That can't be. You've made it clear you're not interested in marriage.'

How bizarre that sounded. As if there were any circumstances in which *she* could ever be courted by a king. From bastard tomboy with skinned knees and prickly pride to royal bride via a career in martial arts and close protection? Not even Hollywood would take on such an outlandish story.

'That doesn't mean I'm not interested in you.' His eyes glowed in a way that made heat squirm through Cat's insides and her breath catch. 'Interest doesn't do justice to what I feel. I want you, Cat. Want you so badly I ache. Just standing here, not touching you, hurts.' He stopped, hefting in a huge breath that lifted his powerful chest against his plain black T-shirt. 'Tell me you feel it too.'

She opened her mouth to tell him she didn't know what he was talking about then snapped it shut.

The same ache rode low in her belly, tightening internal muscles and tensing her thighs.

The only times she'd lied in her life were when she'd taken this job and in her youth when she'd denied the identity of her royal father. That had been for her mother's sake. Her gentle mother had never been able to shrug off the cruelty meted out to her by the townspeople and most especially the man who'd been paid to marry her yet subsequently treated her like dirt.

Her mother who'd fallen in love with a king, who had seduced and abandoned her.

She'd just been a passing fancy to a jaded man. When she'd inconveniently got pregnant the King had bundled her out of her job at the palace before the Queen or anyone else could learn of the affair. As for contacting her later to learn about their child...there'd been utter silence.

How often had Cat heard her stepfather predict she'd come to a bad end? *The apple doesn't fall far from the tree*, he'd say, leering at her, or more often backhanding her across the cheek when she dared defy him or stick up for her beloved mother.

'Cat?' Alex's low, rich voice sent longing shivering through her.

Was this how her mother had felt all those years ago? Overwhelmed by an instant, irrevocable attraction?

Her mother had called it love but Cat wasn't a romantic. This was lust, blazing hot and terrifying because she'd never before experienced anything that so threatened her self-possession. Even the time she'd been shot at and again last year when that madman had tried to run her over with his car.

Cat had been calm, her brain in control of a body trained to disarm any threat.

But not a threat like this.

'Don't say any more!' She heaved a breath into tight lungs. 'I don't want to hear.' She spun away.

'Blocking your ears won't make the truth go away.' His tone wasn't cajoling but serious, almost sympathetic, as if he understood her internal battle.

'Nothing is going to happen between us.' She had to use all her self-control not to swing around and look at him. 'Now, if you'll excuse me, I'll finish my run. Alone.'

Her legs were leaden but she forced herself to run, increasing her pace as she followed the coastal track.

Yet, no matter how fast her pace, Cat couldn't outrun Alex's voice in her head saying he ached for her, or the tension still drawing her limbs tight and stiff.

She'd never been promiscuous. Her mother's fall from grace probably had a lot to do with that, but frankly she'd rarely met a man who attracted her enough.

But with Alex, *King* Alex, the one man it would be utterly catastrophic to get mixed up with, her libido was a raging fire, incinerating doubts, caution and logic.

She couldn't do that to Amelie, even if her half-sister was a stranger and always would be. Cat couldn't sleep with the man Amelie was thinking of marrying.

But was she?

Cat hadn't found out where Amelie was, except that neither she nor her nephew Sébastien were at the palace. Lady Enide had spoken of a private holiday while they recovered from losing King Michel and Queen Irini. Surely if Amelie was going to marry Alex she'd be here.

More—according to Alex, they'd never met. How could Amelie be serious about a marriage?

But there's not going to be a marriage.

Alex had made that absolutely clear. He would leave next week and never return. He and Amelie wouldn't marry. They wouldn't even see each other.

Which meant he'd never discover that Amelie and Cat weren't the same woman.

The thought struck like lightning out of a clear sky, jolting her to a stop, chest heaving and legs shaky from the long sprint. Cat braced her hands on her knees and bent, sucking in great draughts of salty, pine-scented air.

She could accept Alex's offer of an affair, knowing she wasn't hurting Amelie or wrecking her chances with him. Knowing that within a week he'd walk away and so would she. Their paths would never cross again.

What harm could there be in a fling? In giving in and letting this blaze of attraction burn itself out?

Cat grimaced, recognising the voice of temptation. She was stronger than that. For a long time inner strength had been all she possessed. And a determination not to let her illegitimacy make her accept second best.

She fumbled in her pocket for a spare hair tie and wound it round her thick, wavy hair, feeling more like herself with her face bare.

If she'd known she was going to meet Alex she'd have straightened her hair. But it wasn't the first time he'd seen her with it curling around her shoulders. She could only hope he assumed Amelie straightened her hair for every public photo.

Maybe if she concentrated more on pretending to be her sister Cat could thrust aside this terrible, thrumming need. Forget Alex with his *come-to-*

me eyes and engaging smile. And how he'd kissed as if he wanted to consume her.

With a groan of despair, Cat felt her breasts tighten and her feminine core soften.

Forgetting Alex and his proposition was impossible. She'd have to settle for being strong in the face of adversity. That was her specialty after all.

Sadly, she'd never felt so weak in her life.

CHAPTER FIVE

'NO, THANKS.' CAT shook her head at the offered tray, taut muscles protesting even that small movement.

She was so on edge she was as brittle as old glass. The elegant dress of smoke-grey lace scratched at skin turned hyper-sensitive and she had to fight not to shift restlessly in unfamiliar stockings and heels. The string of flawless pearls at her throat felt heavy, as if protesting their use by an imposter.

After avoiding Alex all day, she'd found herself unable to escape dinner with him. Lady Enide hadn't been happy about it but even she conceded they couldn't leave their guest to eat alone.

'You don't like oysters?' he murmured as he helped himself.

Cat shuddered and looked away from the shell in his hand. 'Shellfish allergy.' The memory of her trauma as a child when she'd thought she'd never breathe again was still fresh.

Sympathy tinted his look. 'I won't ask how you discovered that. I understand it can be frightening.'

Cat nodded. 'You can say that again.'

'Do you—?'

'Your Highness.' Lady Enide leaned forward, her smile making her look like a grimacing horse. 'I hear Bengaria will be hosting a new international car race next year. How are plans proceeding for that? It must be very exciting.'

Despite her nerves at the charade she played, and at being so near Alex, Cat fought not to smile. Enide, with her silver hair and severe formality, looked like she belonged in another era. As if her idea of excitement was a new blend of Oolong for high tea with a group of other matrons. Not the deafening roar and blood-pumping adrenaline of motor sports.

But Enide was doing her gallant best to deflect any *tête-à-têtes* between Alex and Cat. Cat was grateful. Every time she met Alex's eyes, or felt his gaze settle appraisingly on her, fear notched taut as a garrotte, stopping the flow of small talk she tried desperately to maintain.

It was a relief to turn to the diplomat on her other side. A youngish man who seemed perfectly at ease. Cat assumed he knew about her deception and was part of the scheme to make it a success. He seemed suave and safe, unremarkable compared with Alex's striking looks and character. There was no lightning bolt of attraction whenever *he* looked at her.

The evening wore on, with the handful of guests taking turns to deflect Alex's attention. Yet they were only partly successful. Though Alex responded adroitly to every conversational gambit, charming even stiff-necked old ladies, Cat knew he watched her with a gaze that bordered on predatory.

Yet what terrified her wasn't the possibility he'd discover her true identity. It was that for the first time in her life she felt the urge not to fight on but to surrender. To accept this terrible yearning and let it run its course.

Madness, sheer madness!

Cat pushed her chair out from the table, on her feet before she could have second thoughts. 'I'm sorry but I must excuse myself.'

The men at the table hurriedly rose and across from her Lady Enide's features took on a pinched look that indicated Cat's manners were appalling.

'I hope you'll forgive me.' Cat's look encompassed the guests, skating past Alex before it could settle. 'I'm afraid I feel rather unwell.' It wasn't a lie. She was sick to the stomach at this duplicitous game and the tight way her hair had been styled gave her a headache. 'Lady Enide, you'll act as hostess in my absence?' It emerged as a statement, not a question, and Enide nodded, looking shocked at Cat's authoritative tone.

That was another reason this masquerade grated. Cat was used to being in control, assessing threats and dealing with them, an expert in her field. Being continually on the back foot, judged as less than capable by everyone, except Alex, didn't suit her.

Cat turned, only to find him beside her, his dark brows furrowing in a V of concern. Between them, out of sight of the rest of the guests, his hand claimed hers and a little jolt of energy shot up her arm.

Their eyes met and power arced between them, tugging her towards him. She made herself resist, but couldn't look away.

'Do you need anything?' His thumb stroked hers in a circular, soothing caress.

Silently she shook her head. Ridiculously, the tenderness in his tone made her throat close over a hot tide of emotion.

This was stupid. There was nothing between them but sexual attraction.

Yet his concern spoke to a part of her she'd forgotten existed. The girl who'd hidden her need for affection since childhood, when she'd witnessed her stepfather's anger whenever her mother dared to cuddle her or show her tenderness. The man had never got over the fact his wife hadn't borne him a child, so he was left with only another man's castoff bastard to raise.

Cat swallowed and slid her hand free. 'I'll be okay after a good sleep,' she lied. Then, with a strained smile, she hurried out the door.

Though she tried, sleep was impossible. Cat was stuck, caught by her devil's bargain with the Prime Minister. If she pulled out he'd ruin her and she'd be in debt for the rest of her life. If she stayed...

She squeezed her eyes shut, wondering how long she could keep up this charade when all it took was the stroke of Alex's hand to make her want—

No! She refused to think about it. Instead she turned to something that always calmed her—physical activity. There was a pool on this side of the palace, screened by hedges. Minutes later she padded barefoot along a paved garden path. Only the faint swish of the sea and the rustle of a bird in a nearby tree broke the silence. It was well past midnight. The guests had gone and the palace was silent. She had the garden to herself.

Cat reached the pool terrace and dropped her robe on flagstones still slightly warm from the day's sun. She hadn't packed a swimming costume and wore the bikini Alex had provided. The memory of his stare when he'd seen her in it sent a shiver through her, making her wrap her arms around herself, suddenly self-conscious.

Cat didn't have hang-ups about her body. It was fit and streamlined. It did what she wanted. She rarely thought of how a man might view it. Now, suddenly, she was wondering if her breasts were too small, her...

'Enough!' she growled and strode across to flick off the underwater lights.

Blackness blanketed the terrace and she looked up, eyes adjusting till she found herself staring at a brilliant wash of stars across the velvet sky. That was better. She'd swim in starlight, lose herself in the rhythm of her stroke, drive herself till exhaustion washed everything from her brain so she could sleep.

One lap became two, became twenty, and Cat's pace didn't slow. She felt the tension drain, the deep-in-her-stomach ripple of sexual desire ease, the knotty problems filling her brain fade as she drove herself through the water, enjoying the familiar feeling that here, now, she was in control.

As she approached the end of the pool she sensed a change. She grabbed the tiled edge and lifted her head, flicking water from her face.

'Hello, Cat.' The deep voice came from the corner of the pool. Instantly her hard-won peace disintegrated. Tension hugged her, drawing every sinew and muscle tight.

'Alex? What are you doing here?'

He moved closer with an easy stroke that ate up the space between them. 'I couldn't sleep. I thought a swim might relax me.'

Cat bit down a retort that he'd followed her. Maybe it *was* true. 'I'll leave you to it.' She put her hands on the edge, ready to lever herself from the water.

'No. Don't go.' The urgency in his tone made her pause, muscles tense in mid-movement. 'Don't run away.'

Cat sank back into the warm water.

She never ran away. She prided herself on facing problems head-on. First her stepfather, then the schoolyard bullies, then starting from scratch in a new country. She'd been a fighter all her life, driven by pride, obstinacy and the belief that, despite what the world thought, she had nothing to be ashamed of simply because of the accident of her birth.

'I've finished my laps.'

In the dim light she saw him shake his head. 'No. You were still going strong till you realised I was here.' He paused. 'I don't want to chase you away.'

Cat's hand tightened on the pool's edge as she caught the gleam of his eyes on her. Her body hummed with excitement, being close to him.

This was dangerous. She spent her professional life protecting people from danger. Every instinct screamed that she needed to leave. If not for her sake, then for Alex's. For Amelie's. Because this was a tangled mess which would unravel into disaster if she wasn't careful.

'This isn't a good idea.' She was turning away when he smiled. Even in the gloom she caught the flash of his grin. Its impact shot straight to her belly.

'Can't we forget everything for half an hour and swim? We don't even need to speak,' he cajoled. 'We'll be Cat and Alex, burning off unwanted energy.'

Cat paused, knowing she should move.

'Come on, Cat. Let go for half an hour. I promise not to tell Lady Frosty. Anyway, you owe me for leaving me with her this evening.'

Despite herself, a giggle bubbled up at his description of Lady Enide. It suited her perfectly.

Cat watched as Alex pushed off from the edge in a long, easy freestyle and somehow, without planning to, she found herself following. His lazy-looking stroke ate up the distance and she had to concentrate to keep up.

Relief filled her, and elation. He was as good as his word, not hassling her with questions, or invading her space. Simply keeping her company as she lost herself in the rhythm of the swim.

Except, even as she entered that almost meditative state of steady exertion, she was aware of his long body cleaving the water beside her, the soft splashes and the arc of his powerful arms as he picked up pace.

It dawned on her that he was pulling ahead, cutting faster through the inky water. Cat quickened speed, determined to catch him.

Up and down the pool they went, he using his superior size and strength to lengthen the gap between them, Cat catching up at every tumble turn with a burst of sheer energy and superior technique.

Finally, when she thought her lungs would explode, Alex slammed to a stop at the pool's end. She slapped her hand against the tiles a couple of seconds later.

'You're quick.' He panted. 'Quick enough to have been a professional.'

She nodded, pulling air into burning lungs. 'Thanks.'

She heaved in another breath, ridiculously delighted at his praise. Despite her swimming talent, there'd been no money when she was young for training, and after she left St Galla she'd had to support herself. Professional swimming couldn't do that so she'd had to abandon that dream. 'So are you.'

'I was fresh and you weren't.' She heard him draw another deep breath. 'And I've got the advantage of being bigger and stronger.'

Cat turned, one hand anchoring her to the pool edge. As she watched he rose, broad, straight shoulders sluicing water like some legendary sea god emerging from the depths. His face was in shadow but she made out the magnificent V shape of his torso, the masculine beauty of his body.

She was so busy staring it took a moment to re-alise they were at the shallow end and he'd risen to his feet.

Feeling foolish, glad of the darkness hiding her expression, she dropped her feet to the tiled floor and stood.

As she did she realised her error. They were no longer separated by distancing water. With the water sliding around her hips she felt a waft of air, a sweet-scented night breeze that, despite its warmth, prickled her skin and turned her nipples to hard points.

Or maybe it wasn't the breeze. Maybe it was Alex. She heard his sigh, watched his shoulders dip and hitch as he drew another breath, and felt his gaze on her. Her skin tingled as if he touched her.

That was bad. Shockingly bad. Yet it felt—

He brushed a lock of saturated hair over her shoulder and Cat shivered, not from cold but from the riot of sensations cascading from his touch.

'I have to go.' It didn't sound like her voice. It was thick and husky. Reluctant.

'I won't hurt you, Cat. I'd never do that.'

He thought she was scared of him? The idea was so appalling she didn't stop to censor her response. 'Of course you wouldn't.' In the short time she'd known him she'd realised he was a good man. Patient, decent, but with a wicked sense of humour and a lethal sexiness that would undo her if she didn't leave *now.*

Abruptly she turned towards the end of the pool just as he stretched out his other hand. He'd been reaching for her arm but now accidentally grazed her breast.

They froze.

Dimly Cat heard the soft trill of a night bird over the thundering pulse in her ears. She sucked in a desperate breath but that only made her breast rise against his open palm, her nipple budding tighter at that gentle scrape.

There was a moment, a long, infinite-seeming moment of stillness. Then a sigh, his or hers, she didn't know, as his fingers curled around her breast, gentle yet sure and possessive, and her eyes fluttered shut.

Just a second longer. A second to conquer the potent pleasure of his touch there. She squeezed her thighs together, trying to stop the pooling heat between her legs and the hollow ache that throbbed deep inside.

'Cat.' It was a groan. She felt a shudder rip through him, his touch tightening on her breast.

Shock held her unmoving—it was so good. 'Cat. Tell me you feel this too.'

'I shouldn't,' she breathed, trying to ignore the glory that was his touch on her body. 'I can't.' Her brain buzzed with all the reasons this was wrong.

'But you do.' His voice was closer and she felt his breath on her bare skin. She snapped her eyes open to find him leaning close. 'You can't pretend about this, Cat. This is about you and me, Alex and Cat. Not diplomatic arrangements.'

Cat looked up into the darkness that was his face, her imagination filling all the details as if she saw him in a spotlight. That high forehead and sweep of black hair. Straight brows, proud nose and glinting, humour-filled eyes. Though there was no humour now. Tension radiated from him, and purpose. His other hand slid down from her shoulder, burning a sizzling trail till he reached her hand and captured it, threading his fingers through hers.

'You want me.'

Cat swallowed.

'Say it, Cat.' His other hand lifted from her breast and she had to stifle a cry of protest. Yet she couldn't prevent herself leaning in, instinctively seeking more.

She was rewarded with the touch of one finger, lightly circling her nipple in a slow, devastatingly seductive caress. Cat went into meltdown and there was nothing she could do to prevent it. She grabbed at the side of the pool with rigid fingers, her other hand gripping his so hard it shook.

'Cat!'

Finally, trembling with the effort, she admitted the truth. 'I want you, Alex.' It was torture and bliss to admit it. 'I've wanted you from the first.'

Powerful arms swept her close to his big, rigid body and his head dropped to her neck, his voice raw as he muttered something in his own language. It sounded anguished, like a man in extremis.

Cat wrapped her arms around him, absorbing the fiery heat beneath his cool, slick skin, burrowing closer to the wall of muscle and bone that made her senses overload in sheer delight.

It was an embrace of comfort as much as desire. For the tension humming between them made even breathing hurt. Cat was bombarded with impressions, her skin hyper-sensitised to the brush of his flesh against hers, the caress of his lips at the base of her throat, the solid weight of his thigh between hers.

She didn't intend to but suddenly her hips were

tilting up, drawing her tight against him so she rode his thigh as she'd imagined riding him.

'Cat.' One hand tugged her head back, then his mouth was on hers and it was as if they'd known each other an eternity. As if that kiss by the sea hadn't ended. As if this was how they were meant to be.

His big body was impossibly familiar, and the taste of him, tangy and addictive, made her hungry for more. The lap of warm water against overheated skin only heightened the sensuality of his embrace. She slid her hands up and down his back, tracing the ripple of muscles, the slick arch of his back, right down to the taut curves of his backside. Her fingers dug in hard as his hands cupped her bottom, lifting her so she felt the rampant swell of his erection.

Heat doused her. Then, before she could recover, he nipped the sensitive flesh where her shoulder curved into her neck and Cat shuddered as a wave of ecstasy took her.

'Alex!' Was that will-o'-the-wisp voice hers? 'We mustn't...'

She slipped her hands around his hips and up his heaving chest, intending to push him away. But somehow the racing thud of his heart against her palm distracted her, and the curve of his pectorals, intriguing with the roughness of hair.

His mouth covered hers again and thought dissolved. Cat was lost in a blast of sensual connection. When she came to her hands were anchored on the back of his skull, clasping him tight, wanting to burrow into him. Her back was to the pool wall with her legs hooked over Alex's thighs.

A quick hand tugged at her bikini bottom, yanking the fabric aside in the water and there he was, searingly hot, bare and virile and perfect. She hadn't been aware of him shucking his swim shorts. Yet she wasn't shocked. For this was what she craved. She tilted her hips and sheet lightning lit the darkness behind her closed lids.

Alex groaned her name, the sound vibrating through his chest to hers as if they were already joined. He kissed her hard, pushing her against the tiles and she kissed him right back, shifting restlessly as he explored the slick flesh he'd exposed between her legs. A pulse beat there, urgent and needy, as he feathered a caress across her most sensitive spot and she jolted in his embrace.

His touch slid lower, deeper, probing, and Cat thought she'd explode with wanting. She needed him *now*.

She slipped her hand between them, encircling

his thick length, exulting in the way he twitched in her hold, his hips bucking up against her. Another dazzle of lightning, another—

A firm hand loosened her grasp, pushing her away. Before she could protest he was there, nudging her entrance, hot and bold and—

'Yes!' Did she gasp it out loud or merely think it? Cat didn't know or care. All she cared about was the perfection of his long, slow thrust of power right to her core. She wanted to revel in it, to rejoice and savour every sensation. But already the tumult was upon her.

It began as a ripple of delight up her backbone. A tingle of pleasurable friction through her body where he filled her. Then the ripple became a wave, a surge of delight so intense she had to dig her nails into him as the tide threatened to sweep her away.

But then Alex moved. He pulled back then bucked forward, hip to hip, filling her to a point she'd never reached before.

Suddenly the surge was a mighty rip current, sucking her down and out into an ocean of rapture. Waves crashed and thundered. Lightning struck. She was sure it did. Felt it in the bite of electricity that tingled from her soles to her scalp.

She hung on and prayed it would never end. That she'd survive intact.

It was the single most glorious, frightening, wonderful experience of her life.

Alex lowered her to the wide day-bed, falling half over, half beside her, their bodies super-heated from sexual satisfaction.

It should have been impossible for him to walk, much less carry Cat out of the shallows and over the flagstones into the pool house. In the pool it had felt as if his bones as well as his muscles had dissolved in that shattering climax. He should be floating, boneless with satiation.

Except Cat had collapsed against him, murmuring snatches of fractured French against his neck, nuzzling him as if she couldn't get close enough. Exhaustion had vanished as his body quickened again.

He couldn't remember needing a woman so voraciously. Once had been nowhere near enough. Whatever the explanation for this stark hunger, Alex knew it would take more than a quickie to sate. He doubted even a week sharing her bed would be enough. But he was willing to try. So willing.

Already his erection lay heavy along her thigh. His naked erection.

Hell! Alex rolled away just as Cat opened her eyes.

'We didn't use a condom!' Dismay roughened her voice as she made the same realisation.

Their eyes met. Despite the horror surging through him at the thought of unprotected sex, Alex felt again that gut-deep throb of desire.

'I'm sorry.' His voice was so thick he could barely get the words out. 'I didn't think.'

He shook his head. *Unbelievable!* Guilt and disbelief slammed him. Thirty-two and he'd acted like a reckless kid.

He was *never* reckless. He took risks, calculated risks, especially in the years when he'd been a test pilot for experimental jets. But he was never stupid. 'I've never had unprotected sex in my life.'

Yet to his chagrin saying the words made him remember how magnificent sex with Cat, utterly naked and unprotected, had been. To add to his confusion, he realised it wasn't the lack of a condom that made the difference. It was Cat. Cat and him together.

'Neither have I.' Her stunned eyes held his, making him want to reassure her. Her jaw firmed. 'I don't sleep around so you're not in danger from me. And I'm on the Pill for other reasons, so there won't be a pregnancy.'

It took a moment for Alex to process her words. He was stuck trying to hold himself back from touching her again. When he did take in her meaning, relief hit full force. 'Then we're both safe.'

He gave in then to the compulsion to touch, stroking her cheek and watching her eyes flutter closed.

The shock of having unprotected sex should have quenched his desire. That alone should make him pause and rethink what was happening here.

Instead all he felt was renewed urgency.

'Cat.' Her eyes snapped open, holding his. His hand paused in its rhythmic caress. Again that shimmer of heat passed between them, as powerful as a seismic quake. He had no name for it. No explanation.

An inner voice of caution told him to beware, to walk away and take the time to dissect these unprecedented sensations.

Caution be damned.

'Are you okay?'

She nodded. 'I've never behaved this way.' She swallowed and something inside Alex squeezed hard at her distress. Just as another part of him discovered her pale, slim throat was mouth-wateringly seductive.

He pressed his lips to the base of her neck, tasting her trembling pulse.

'I haven't either. You probably won't believe it but I'm never careless.' A childhood spent under his father's roof had seen to that. His father had liked nothing better than exploiting weakness. As a result Alex had grown up utterly self-contained, only learning to relax and enjoy life when he'd left Bengaria.

Cat nodded, the movement jerky. 'Me too.' She swallowed again. 'This... I can't explain what happened.'

Alex let his hand slide down her damp skin to her collarbone. She had a sensual allure that spiked his attempts to regroup and think this through.

With Cat he felt elemental longing, an urge to meld himself with her in the most primitive way possible.

'Pheromones,' he suggested gravely, knowing the answer, if there was an answer, was more than that.

A hint of a smile caught the edges of her lush mouth and heat pooled in Alex's belly.

'Biorhythms?' she offered. 'Hormones?' She

sighed and his attention dropped to the rise of her breasts, barely covered by the skimpy bikini.

'Abstinence,' he whispered, enthralled as he skimmed his hand over the saturated fabric and felt the taut nub of her nipple tickle his palm.

'You could be right,' she sighed, arching her back, pushing her breast into his hand.

'It's been a while?'

'Years.' She sucked in her breath as he stroked his thumb across her nipple. He loved the answering jolt of response that passed through her, making her body taut with longing.

'Me too.'

'Really?' Her eyes rounded in astonishment and he'd have laughed out loud if sexual tension wasn't clamping every muscle tight.

'Really.' Their gazes held and it was like the unseen but palpable backdraft of a fire, sucking them both closer.

She swallowed, her hand clamping his wrist. He felt the strength of her grip and remembered the clean, athletic way she'd cut through the water. The way she'd gripped him with her legs as they'd come together.

'Not a good idea.'

Alex shook his head. 'Sorry?'

'We should stop. Now.'

Alex knew he should be thanking her. Far from reading too much into what had happened, she was telling him their tryst was over.

'Are you involved with someone else?' As he asked it, he tasted sourness on his tongue. He didn't want marriage, but he discovered a streak of jealousy at the thought of Cat with another man.

'I told you, there's no one.' Her brow puckered and to his surprise he found even that endearing.

'In that case—' he lifted his thigh over her hip '—there's no reason we shouldn't enjoy ourselves.'

She firmed her mouth and he knew she was going to argue, despite the way she shifted eagerly beneath him.

Alex stifled her protest, stroking his tongue along her lips once, twice. He was rewarded on the third stroke when she opened for him, sucking his tongue deep into the sensual haven of her mouth.

Alex slid his hand to her bikini bottom he hadn't bothered to remove in the pool, only to find his fingers tangling with hers as she wrenched at the slick fabric.

Satisfaction and anticipation pulsed through him. It was going to be a long, delightful night.

CHAPTER SIX

ALEX SAT ON his balcony, feeling the early sun on limbs that were lethargic after a night's energetic loving. A smile widened his mouth as well-being enveloped him.

Clearly he shouldn't have abstained from sex so long, despite his taxing workload and the fact most women seemed attracted as much by the glamour of his title as by him. Glamour! Repairing the damage his father had done to the country by selling national assets for his own gain and favouring cronies in shonky deals. Despite the pomp and glitter, Alex hadn't found much glamour in being royal.

Cat changed that. Though *glamour* wasn't quite the word. Exciting was more like it. She was classy and sexy in a way that had nothing to do with court protocol or public show.

Her allure cut through the red tape surrounding them. He'd responded to it the morning they'd met and again last night. He'd been charmed by her directness. And something he couldn't name—a quality that made her stand out.

That was why, after saying goodbye to her half an hour ago, he was sitting watching the sun come up, searching the Net for information on her. Not the information his mother and his advisers had provided, focused on her family ties and official work.

After a night in her arms, a night of the best sex in his life, he needed to know more. Last night, away from the hangers-on who chaperoned them, he'd glimpsed the real Princess Amelie.

He mightn't want to marry her but he needed... more.

A huff of laughter escaped as he hit enter on his laptop. Okay, he wanted more sex with her. He wanted a flaming affair that would last as long as he was here, hopefully burning out the compulsion he felt for her by the time he left.

The connection between them was unprecedented. They'd spent the night exploring each other's bodies. They should have been limp with exhaustion. Yet when they'd parted downstairs they'd devoured each other all over again, Cat with her back to the wall and her fingernails digging into his shoulders and he with his hand between her legs and his body aflame.

He was hard now, wishing he'd followed her to her suite instead of returning to his.

Alex surveyed the images he'd found. In every photo she looked charming and well-groomed, with that lovely smile and perfect poise. He preferred her passionate and naked beneath him. And her hair. Why bother straightening it for every public appearance? He enjoyed the way it curled around his hand as if it had a life of its own. It was sexy, like Cat herself.

As ever, Alex was struck by the difference between the woman in the photos and the one he knew. It was something indefinable, but nevertheless real. Strange he should feel it with every picture he found.

He scrolled, looking for something more informal. And suddenly there she was, not smiling but grinning. It was another official event and she was dressed to the nines but the photographer had caught her in a moment of genuine delight as she lifted something to her mouth.

Alex clicked on the link and discovered a short piece about her opening a local seafood festival. There was a blessing of the boats with feasting and—

He blinked and backtracked, rereading the text.

A cloud must have covered the sun for a chill ran through him, dousing the warmth of sexual gratification and lazy expectation.

Alex sat straighter, searching for a simple explanation and knowing there was none. Not an honest one.

His gut tightened and his jaw clamped. He detested deception. He'd lived with it all his life. To outsiders his parents' marriage had been loving and stable. Only those caught within had known his father Cyrill had been an unfeeling autocrat, showing a smiling face to the world while he made his wife and son's lives hell.

As Regent, Cyrill had managed Bengaria for his own ends. Then he'd undermined Alex's cousin, Stefan, when he'd come of age and inherited the throne. He'd bullied Stefan's sister, Marisa, when she wouldn't kowtow to him. And when Stefan died he'd pretended grief while systematically pillaging the country's wealth for his own gratification.

Alex frowned. His father cast a long shadow, but he was dead and gone. This deception was about Cat.

No, not about Cat, but *by* her.

There was a buzzing in his ears, a fullness in his

chest as he thought of the woman he'd made love to all night—so honest in her desire, so open and generous. The woman he'd connected with as no other. Deceiving him.

He looked at the photo of her grinning as she lifted an oyster to her lips.

Shellfish allergy. That was what she'd said last night.

Which meant the woman in the photo couldn't be Cat.

Cat wasn't Princess Amelie.

She even had to straighten her hair to play the part, he realised. No wonder she didn't quite look like her photos!

Anger, the slow-burning sort that hadn't ignited since his father's death, sparked deep inside. He'd spent his early years manipulated by a ruthless liar. He'd believed he could identify deception better than most, yet still he'd been taken in. Taken in and made a fool of.

She'd listened as he'd all but apologised for not wanting to marry. Worse, he realised with a prickle of foreboding, he'd spilled family secrets. Believing her to be Amelie, he'd revealed the truth of his parents' marriage.

His mother had found precious little happiness

in marriage but still had her pride. The idea he'd blurted her private pain to someone who might sell the story to the press was untenable.

The photo of the smiling woman before him blurred as a red mist descended.

Cat slipped her feet into the elegant shoes that matched the hyacinth-blue dress. If only it were as easy to put on the persona of a princess as to wear these beautiful clothes.

But Cat didn't feel like a gracious royal. She didn't even feel like herself this morning. Her skin was tight, her pulse too quick as excitement effervesced in her blood.

She hadn't slept, yet instead of exhaustion she felt invigorated by a night spent sharing her body with a stranger.

A man who believed she was her half-sister.

Her stomach dipped and she pressed a hand to it, as if she could prevent the welling emotions. Worry, shame and, despite those, excitement. For last night had been unlike anything she'd experienced. What she'd felt with Alex…

She pulled herself up. She couldn't go there. Instead she surveyed herself in the mirror: a fake royal, right down to the carefully straightened hair and high heels she'd never have chosen for herself.

She had no right to think about the joy of her stolen night with Alex. For it *had* been stolen.

Would he have slept with her if he'd known who she was? Logic said no. Yet her heart hoped.

Hoped what? That there was a way around this horrible mess? That somehow they'd find a way to connect again, not just sexually, but—

'No.' Saying it aloud shut down her circling thoughts.

But it didn't stop the regret. She'd done wrong, withholding the truth. Even if he didn't plan to marry Amelie, he deserved to know who he'd been with, and who she wasn't.

The knowledge of what she had to do was a weight dragging at her belly, making her wish she could stay in her room and not face him. But it had to be done. Pride, fighting spirit, call it what you will—she'd always faced problems head-on. It was one of the reasons her bullying stepfather had hated her—she'd stood up for what she believed was right. It was the way she was made and she couldn't change now.

It was one thing to keep her role here a secret.

It was something else, something sordid and unpleasant, to deceive Alex after last night.

Cat set her chin, spun on one spindly heel and walked to the door.

'Alex?' Despite herself she couldn't keep the excitement from her voice, or repress the anticipation curling her insides tight.

He swung round, silhouetted against the huge windows at the end of the room. Cat's mouth dried as she took in his long-legged, wide-shouldered form. Last night she'd explored every inch of him with an unfamiliar hunger that hadn't abated. She could still taste the warm tang of his flesh on her tongue. The sense memory weakened her knees.

Cat had never thought of herself as a sensual woman, but last night had been an eye-opener. She'd never craved a man like she'd craved Alex. The way she still did.

She couldn't read his expression but felt his eyes on her and that was enough. Her nipples puckered and between her legs she felt a lick of damp heat. Nervously she clenched her muscles, trying to regain control.

'Princess.'

Her brows gathered close. Of all the outrageous

things he'd called her last night, that hadn't been one of them. How grateful she was. The word was a reminder of all that lay between them.

Cat swallowed and forced herself to walk slowly towards him. She wanted to kick off the spindly heels and run barefoot to him. To launch herself, confident that he'd catch her and sweep her up for a kiss.

Except she didn't have that right. She wasn't who he thought. She needed to get the truth off her chest. Surely she could rely on his discretion not to let the Prime Minister know she'd revealed the secret of her identity.

Her heart beat too high, as if it had leapt into her throat.

'Will you—?'

'We need to talk.' He sounded tense.

Cat peered at him, trying to make out his expression against the light. He didn't sound like the same man she'd made love to through the night. Maybe lack of sleep made him grumpy.

'Yes, we do. I was about to ask if you'd walk with me in the garden.' If they went now they'd avoid Lady Enide and have a chance of privacy.

'Lead the way, my lady.' His tone, and the way he called her *my lady* instead of Cat or even Amelie, sent anxiety skating down her backbone. Or maybe it was the fact he made no move to touch her—so different from last night when he couldn't get enough of her.

Cat squashed disappointment and turned to the door. 'This way.'

Silently she led him outside, down gravelled paths and past mirror pools that reflected the azure sky and pale pink palace with its delicate white frosting of decorative work. Past fountains and the knot garden and the rose arbour, heavy with scent. Through the French garden and the Italian garden to the secluded nook she'd discovered that wasn't overlooked.

A waft of salty air teased her nostrils as she sank onto the bench overlooking the forest and the gleaming Mediterranean. Cat turned, drawing a fortifying breath.

Alex stood, arms crossed, legs planted wide. Despite his tailored jacket and trousers and his crisp cotton shirt, he looked dangerous rather than suave. His eyes were stormy not laughing, his mouth thin-lipped and jaw clenched.

She blinked. She'd never seen him like this. 'Alex? What's wrong?'

A voice inside told her she was delaying because

once she told him the truth there'd be no more smiles. No more intimacy.

'What could be wrong?' Yet his voice was as tight as the muscles bunching beneath his sleeves. It reminded her of what she'd discovered last night. That he was potently masculine, with a powerful body that made her glad she was a woman.

Cat sucked in air, trying to focus. 'You seem... different today.'

'Really? Not what you expected?' He lifted his eyebrows. 'I could say the same of you.'

'Sorry?' Cat froze on the bench seat. Something was wrong. She had such a bad feeling.

He tilted his head as if to get a better view of her. Yet he'd already seen more of her than anyone in the world.

'You can stop the innocent act. It makes me sick. All I want is the truth. Who the hell are you?'

Cat gaped. 'You know?' Yet hadn't she known she'd never fool anyone?

What had given her away? Did it matter? The fact was he knew. It was there in his scornful stare.

'That you're not who you pretend?' His nostrils flared and he looked down his straight, well-bred nose with all the hauteur of his aristocratic ancestors.

This time his searing stare didn't sizzle so much as slice at her unprotected flesh. Gone was last night's ardent lover, gone the charismatic man whose humour and potent sex appeal had drawn her into behaving totally out of character.

Cat shivered, her hands running up her bare arms as they prickled.

What had she expected?

'I was going to tell you—'

'Really?' One slashing eyebrow lifted in patent disbelief.

'Yes!' She shot to her feet then didn't know what to do with herself. She wanted to reach out to him, bridge the gulf widening between them. But that was impossible. The man surveying her wasn't the man she'd fallen for so hard and fast. He was an imperious stranger. 'That's why I wanted to talk with you privately. To explain.'

'Explain away then, Ms…?'

'Dubois. Cat Dubois.'

'So Cat is your real name?' Even now he sounded disbelieving.

'Catherine. But I don't use my full name. I've been Cat for years.' Since she'd escaped this country. It had been her mother's pet name for her, the one remaining link she had to the sweet woman taken too early by cancer.

Besides, Cat suited her more. Catherine was gentle and delicate, like her mother—so feminine and beautiful. Cat was strong and independent. As for femininity, that was something she'd spent her life downplaying. It had been her mother's downfall and in Cat's job it was a definite negative when people wanted someone to protect them.

Alex said nothing, merely stared stonily. She breathed deep, regret knotting her insides. Regret and guilt. She should have told him. Should never have let herself be swept away.

Shame bit. Had she let herself go because she'd known he'd never have made love to her if he knew who she really was?

'I was coming to tell you the truth—'

'I'm not interested in what you *meant* to do.' His brusque tone killed off hope he might eventually understand her predicament. 'I want to know who you are and why you conned me.'

Cat nodded and swallowed, trying not to wince when it felt as if her throat was lined with broken glass.

'My name is Cat Dubois and I live in the US. I'm a bodyguard.'

'A bodyguard?' He frowned. 'Princess Amelie's bodyguard?'

'No. I've never met the Princess.' And never would now. Why had she given in to curiosity about her royal relations? She'd been crazy to hope she'd meet them, or understand their world by entering it for a couple of weeks. She looked at Alex's censorious expression, the aggressively bunched arms and tendons taut in his neck, and knew she'd destroyed whatever fragile connection had briefly flared between them. Desolation engulfed her.

'I don't usually work in St Galla.'

'But you're from here.' When she frowned up at him he explained. 'At dinner the other night I heard you speaking with the diplomats. It wasn't pure French but a version I've only heard here.'

Of course he'd know the difference. His French was perfect and cultured. With his privileged upbringing he'd probably been tutored in half a dozen languages.

'I was born on the island, but I haven't lived here for a decade.'

He said nothing and she forced herself to go on, though every word weighed like lead.

'A couple of weeks ago I was approached to do a job here as a body double.' Still not even a flicker in those cool, dark eyes. 'It was an offer too good to refuse.'

Bitterness welled. She'd told herself that with the money she could open the centre for teenagers she'd dreamed of. But it had been her yearning to connect with Amelie that persuaded her. How self-destructive! You'd think she'd have learned years before that a connection with that side of her family could cause only pain.

'You work for the Princess?'

'I told you, I've never met her.' She looked out to sea, preferring the view to his cold eyes. 'Apparently she's…away, I assume with little Prince Sébastien. I was employed to attend a function in her place next week. I've been here learning how to act the part.' Her mouth twisted. She might be able to walk in heels now, just, but, as far as Lady Enide was concerned, she was a hopeless princess.

He said nothing and she swung round, her chin lifting so she could look him in the eye. 'Then out of the blue you turned up. I didn't even know who you were at first. No one mentioned you'd be visiting. If I'd known I had to meet the Princess's fiancé I'd never have taken the job.'

'I'm not her fiancé.' If possible he looked even

more forbidding than before. Cat's shoulders tightened and her skin iced but she stood her ground.

'Almost fiancé then.' Cat bit out the words, reminding herself that was none of her business. She'd had a bone-melting one-night stand with him but that was all. She'd never been in his league and had always known it. 'It's been hard keeping up the pretence of being Amelie with you here.'

'So you decided to sleep with me to distract me from the truth?' Contempt honed his features. If his face grew any tighter he'd be able to use that jaw as a blade.

'Distract you?' Cat couldn't help it. Her voice rose in outrage. Fury was a relief after the shame and nerves that racked her. 'Who did the seducing? Who's the one that wouldn't ignore the…attraction between us?'

Her pulse beat loud as silence stretched between them.

'If you'd told me who you were instead of leading me on—'

'What? If I'd told you I wasn't royal you wouldn't have kissed me, is that it?' Cat couldn't rein in her anger any more. She'd spent half a lifetime weathering the hurts inflicted by others. She'd learned not to show pain. But this…this was a raw, bleeding wound. She'd actually believed there was something special between her and Alex despite coming from different worlds. That he was attracted to her, Cat, the real woman, not the persona she played.

Her hands found her hips and her eyes narrowed on that gorgeous, aristocratic face. 'Because a prince couldn't possibly be attracted to a commoner, could he?'

Except she was wrong. Her father had been a monarch, her mother a maid.

'That's got nothing to do with it.' Fire blazed in his expression and Cat was almost grateful. Facing that cool, condemning stare took more bravery than she'd expected.

'It's got everything to do with it. You'd never have—'

'You're skating on thin ice, Ms Dubois. Don't pretend to know me based on a few hours of sex. You've done nothing but lie since I got here.'

Cat rocked back on her feet, her hands sliding down to clasp in front of her. He was right. She'd stupidly felt there was more to the connection between them. There *was* no connection. He was a virile man and she'd caught his eye. Maybe he'd viewed sex with Amelie as an amusing way to pass the time while stuck here.

For all she knew he had a string of affairs wherever he went. Maybe he was just good at keeping the gossip out of the press.

Cat was torn between horror at her naiveté, shame at her behaviour and despair that even now, confronting his utter contempt, she craved the fantasy she'd let herself believe last night.

She'd never felt so lost.

'Did you lie about being on the Pill too?' His harsh voice grated her nerves. Dully she wondered how deep the degradation could go.

'No.' Once more she looked away, finding no comfort in the gorgeous sea view. 'I take it to manage my cycle.' The erratic, sometimes painful periods had been tough to deal with on some jobs. 'And I don't have any diseases.'

'If I can believe you.'

Cat's shoulders hunched but she said nothing. His doubt made her feel tainted. She'd striven so long to become someone she was proud of. In one night she'd put herself in a position where he diminished her self-worth.

No, not one night. It wasn't all down to him. She shouldn't have accepted this job. She hated deception, even if this masquerade had seemed harmless, actually helping Amelie through a crisis. Cat had betrayed herself as well as Alex.

'So all I have to worry about is a kiss-and-tell story in the press.'

Cat's laugh, an abrasive, husky sound, escaped before she could stop it. 'If you think I'm going to breathe a word about last night, you're completely wrong. I can't think of anything worse than sharing my mistake in public.' The thought sent a shudder down her spine.

'Mistake?'

Cat swung around. Something in his tone was unexpected, something other than disdain and disbelief, but she couldn't identify it.

'Surely that's the one thing we agree on. Last night should never have happened. It was a dreadful mistake.'

She watched emotion cross his face—too fast for her to read. Yet she was left with the impression her words angered him even more.

'You're assuring me you're not interested in blackmail—your silence for a fee? Then there's the chance to sell the press an inside scoop on my parents' marriage. Too good to miss, surely?'

Cat drew herself up so high her taut muscles twanged in protest. 'I'm not in the habit of lying.'

She saw his lip curl and hurried on. 'Which is why I'm not good at it. I won't talk to the press about you *or* your family. I believe in respecting people's privacy. As for money, my contract with the Prime Minister provides more than enough.'

'The Prime Minister?' His eyes narrowed.

Cat hesitated. She shouldn't tell Alex these details. The penalty for discussing her contract was heavy. Yet he knew the main part already. Why prevaricate?

'He hired me to be Amelie for a short time.' She frowned. 'For the period you were expected to visit, in fact. Why would…?' She shook her head. She had enough to worry about without concerning herself with the Prime Minister's reasons. 'He hired me for a substantial fee. I have no interest in getting money from you as well.'

Given the choice, she'd leave the money behind if she could walk away right now. Instinct had been right. She should never have returned. The place was poison to her.

'He told you to have sex with me?' Alex's deep voice was harsh, rougher than she'd ever heard it.

'What sort of woman do you think I am?' Cat wrapped her arms around herself as pain sliced through her middle. She'd thought the shame could get no worse, but she'd been wrong. How could he look at her as if she were something filthy he'd picked up on the bottom of his shoe when a couple of hours ago…?

'Don't answer that.' She hefted a deep breath that smelled of sunshine and pines, the sea and hot male flesh. Longing quivered through her, longing for Alex as he'd been last night—sexy and fun, warm and tender, passionate and generous. Not the man who watched her with disdain. Devastation engulfed her.

'No one told me to have sex with you. It was my own stupid idea. Not that it was an idea,' she muttered. 'If I'd thought about it properly I'd never have done it.'

So she said but she wasn't sure she believed it. She'd been in Alex's thrall from the first, despite her attempts to pretend she wasn't.

'But you kept pushing and pushing.' She was shifting the blame for her weakness but it hadn't all been her fault! 'I kept thinking of the Princess but you insisted you weren't planning to see her again. It wasn't as if I was stopping you and her—'

'So that made it all right? The fact I wasn't planning to marry Amelie meant you felt free to deceive me?' There was such ire in his expression, with another man she'd be concerned he'd turn violent like her stepfather.

But Alex wasn't like that. Cat noted the fact and told herself it meant nothing. He still despised her.

Wearily Cat pressed a hand to her temple. Stress and lack of sleep made her head thump.

'You're right. There's no excuse. I should never have slept with you, no matter what the circumstances.' No matter how her body had been aflame with need. Or that she'd never felt such a response to any other man. 'As for deceiving you, it wasn't honourable. I can only apologise.'

Alex looked down into wide sea-green eyes and realised she'd taken the wind from his sails. His lashing fury stalled in the face of her patent regret.

Regret that she'd spent the night giving him the most intense sexual pleasure of his life.

No, that wasn't what he wanted her to apologise for.

It was the deception he hated. The way she'd played him for a fool. That rankled.

But her frank apology and talk of honour disarmed him. Was that a ploy to deflect his anger?

Damn the woman. He'd revelled in the simplicity of last night's pleasure, only to uncover a murky web of dishonesty. That infuriated him. When he looked at her jaw set hard, her eyes fixed on his as if waiting for punishment and her arms clasped protectively around herself, he wanted to believe everything she said. Believe her and let it go.

'I signed a secrecy clause, you see. The penalty for telling anyone the truth would ruin me financially.' She swallowed. 'I thought I was helping the Princess. I didn't think there'd be anyone else with a...personal interest in my masquerade.'

A personal interest. That was one way of putting it.

The remarkable thing was that, despite this morning's revelations and that sick-to-the-gut feeling of having been duped, Alex was still interested, physically at least.

What did that say about him?

'What happens now?' She dropped her arms, standing like a soldier at attention. In her feminine purple-blue dress and narrow shoes she should have looked ridiculous. Instead something caught in his chest at the sight of her.

'Nothing.' He made a snap decision. 'We continue as before.'

As her eyes bulged he realised she was remembering them together through the night, their slick bodies so attuned that every touch, every taste was bliss.

'You pretend to be Amelie. I pretend to think you are. Under no circumstance are you to tell anyone I know the truth. Or what happened between us.' It was clear this charade had been to fool him and he intended to find out why. 'And you don't breathe a word about my mother to anyone. Understood?'

She nodded but it wasn't enough.

He reached out and gripped her jaw, keeping his touch firm, ignoring the silky invitation of her soft flesh and the hitch in her breath that reminded him how responsive she'd been to his touch.

'If you betray me again you won't just have to worry about a financial penalty. I'll make sure you never work again, in the States or anywhere else.'

CHAPTER SEVEN

'THERE'S BEEN A change of plan. I've been speaking to Monsieur Barthe.'

Cat watched Lady Enide's lips pinch and realised that for once she wasn't the cause of the woman's disapproval. After this morning's confrontation with Alex Cat felt so dreadful she expected to be held responsible for whatever this new problem was. The disdain in Alex's eyes...

'You spoke with the Prime Minister?' Cat moved to the edge of the antique gilt chair. She'd tried to contact him too, to beg him to release her from her contract. She hadn't got past his secretaries.

'Didn't I say so?' Enide snapped. Then she blinked and sat back, looking for the first time old and frail. Her brow puckered. 'I'm sorry, Ms Dubois. I'm finding this situation...more difficult than I'd imagined. That's no excuse for taking it out on you.'

'What did you imagine it would be like?' Cat leaned closer.

The older woman's mouth thinned and she looked at her hands. 'A one-off event to buy the Princess more time…'

'The Princess. Is she all right? They wouldn't tell me.' Despite her own worries, Cat's concern for Amelie rose again. Why would a royal walk away from her life? Her obligations? Especially Princess Amelie—a poster girl for duty and responsibility.

'You care?' Enide swung back, eyes rounding. She stared at Cat as if she'd never seen her.

'I…' It was Cat's turn to look away. She couldn't stifle the belief that Amelie needed her help. 'I've wondered if she's okay. The situation is so odd I can't shake the feeling there's something badly wrong.' Everything pointed to a major crisis if Amelie didn't attend the reception.

A muffled sound of distress made her turn. Enide pressed an embroidered handkerchief to her mouth.

'Lady Enide? Can I get you a glass of water?' Cat rose.

The woman shook her head, indicating with a blue-veined hand that Cat should sit. 'Thank you, but I'm fine. I'm just an emotional old woman.'

After a week of icy stares Cat thought of her as stern, impatient, haughty—not emotional. This was a new side to Lady Enide. 'You care about Princess Amelie.'

'Of course! Her mother was my younger cousin and Amelie is just like her—sweet-natured, caring...'

'And you're worried about her.'

The older woman met her eyes. 'It's been a very difficult time for the family—for Amelie and especially little Sébastien. They desperately need time before they have to face...' she waved her hand to encompass their plush surroundings '...what's required of them.'

Cat frowned. Did she mean resuming their normal life or something more? Instinct said something more.

'You're not what I expected, Ms Dubois. You continually surprise me.'

'I do?' Did Enide suspect what had happened with Alex? Cat's stomach dropped. At the time, being with him had seemed the most natural, beautiful thing that had ever happened to her. But, faced with his fury and caught in this masquerade, Cat wished it had never happened.

'I made assumptions about you based on what I guessed of your background.'

Cat stared at the other woman and was surprised to see her cheeks flush.

'My background?' Her stomach roiled.

'Forgive me, I—'

'What do you know about my background?'

Enide folded her handkerchief in her lap. 'Only what I was told. You were born in the north of the country, your parents ran a bakery, and you now live in the US.'

Her eyes lifted. 'But I remember a young woman from the same town who worked in the palace years ago. Her name was Catherine. Very pretty and popular. Everyone was surprised when she left without explanation. She had a way of tilting her head when thinking, a way of looking at you as if she saw right to your thoughts, that I haven't seen in years. Till now.'

Cat sank back, her chest pounding.

'I knew the old King better than many. His reputation as a devoted husband wasn't what it seemed.'

Cat's insides knotted. Her hands turned clammy. She'd thought no one knew her secret. She'd believed it had died with her mother and stepfather.

'Who else—?'

'No one.' Was that sympathy in the old lady's

eyes? 'You wouldn't have been brought here if anyone suspected.'

Cat looked away. Sympathy was better than the disgust she remembered from childhood, but still it felt invasive, like prodding a hidden bruise. She thought she'd left this behind. The feelings of shame, of being tainted, of being an outsider.

'I apologise, Ms Dubois. I thought at first you were here to make trouble for Amelie.'

Cat's mouth twisted. 'Revenge because she had what I could never have?' There'd definitely been a desire to discover what her half-sister's life was like, maybe even a little envy at having everything handed to her without hardship. 'I'm not like that.'

'I realise that now.'

Cat's eyebrows rose in surprise.

Enide smiled. Her first genuine smile and it transformed her from icy harridan to a careworn woman with surprising warmth. 'I may have been biased but there's nothing wrong with my powers of observation. You've conducted yourself wonderfully in difficult circumstances. It's a daunting task and you've thrown yourself into it without complaint. Even with the complication of King Alex being here.' Her expression sobered. 'And hasn't that disrupted everything?'

'Lady Enide? Why was I brought here?'

The other woman blinked and refocused. 'The Prime Minister is determined Amelie will marry the King of Bengaria. With Amelie…away indefinitely it's possible she wouldn't return in time for next week's celebrations. Which would kill any hope of a royal match since King Alex is here specifically to meet her.' She shook her head. 'Having you here keeps the possibility of a match alive till Amelie returns, even if it means moving heaven and earth to keep you and King Alex at arm's length so he doesn't recognise the deception later.'

Cat's head whirled. 'She hasn't been kidnapped?'

Enide's mouth turned up at the corners. 'She's safe, I promise you. But for once she's setting her own priorities instead of doing what's expected. The powers that be don't know where she is and, even if I knew for sure, I wouldn't betray her.' Her long chin jutted. 'She has other things to concentrate on. She doesn't even know you're here.'

'I see.' Amelie was about her own mysterious business. The authorities were going to extraordinary lengths to promote a marriage between her and Alex—a match Alex had no intention of accepting. It was a tangled mess.

Cat's instinct for self-preservation urged her to walk away and return to her own world.

Except she'd be ruined financially. And Alex had promised to see she never worked again. Did he have the power? She shivered. A black mark against her name by a VIP like Alex would damage her reputation irreparably.

Would he really do it?

'You said there's been a change of plan?'

Enide sighed. 'King Alex has contacted Monsieur Barthe with a list of visits he intends to make. He seems to have decided to end his vacation and turn this stay into a business opportunity. In the circumstances it would appear odd if you don't accompany him on at least some of those visits.'

Nausea rose again. Along with a frisson of excitement that worried her more than anything. Surely, knowing how he felt about her, Cat's attraction to him should have withered?

'You want me to spend time with him? What about the danger of being unmasked?'

'It's unfortunate. But—'

A door snicked open on the other side of the sitting room. 'Ah, there you are, Lady Enide. And Princess Amelie too. How delightful.' Alex's smile was charming. It was only when she met his eyes that Cat read steely anger.

So Cat had her answer. He'd meant every lashing word. She was stuck here, for good or bad.

Ire still seared his belly. Yet as Alex sat with Lady Enide and Cat over afternoon tea, watching the tension in Cat's slim frame and the effort the older woman made to keep the conversation rolling, he felt an unwanted flicker of sympathy for them.

He couldn't understand it. His father's conniving and manipulation had given him an abhorrence for liars. There should *be* no sympathy.

He didn't know what had made Enide take part in this outrageous con. He respected her, not just because of his mother's recommendation but because he'd come to enjoy her incisive observations and dry humour. As for the fake Princess Amelie—the shadows beneath her eyes and the tight line of her mouth made her appear ridiculously vulnerable. He told himself he didn't care.

Yet when she entered the fray, engaging him in conversation when Enide faltered and pressed a hand to her forehead, Alex mentally applauded her grace under pressure. Even when he deliberately turned the conversation to people and places she couldn't know, she didn't back down. With a flash of those stunning eyes she surprised him with her apparently easy answers. She *had* been doing her homework.

What's more, she didn't by so much as a flicker of expression indicate she knew he was deliberately aiming to catch her out. Only the flat quality of her smile betrayed the effort it took to keep up the performance. That and her concern as she watched Lady Enide.

Since when had the pair been friends? That wasn't the vibe he'd got.

Alex didn't know whether to be pleased Cat hadn't collapsed in a heap now he'd confronted her, or concerned at how easily she disguised her true self. Was she really such a consummate liar? Last night he'd have sworn he'd never been with a more honest, open woman.

Before he'd discovered she'd done nothing but lie!

Yet he couldn't ignore that fizz of awareness when she handed him a coffee cup and their fingers brushed. Wildfire raced through his veins and the low cadence of her voice caught at his libido.

'Excuse me, Your Highness, Your Majesty...'

'Yes?' Cat turned to the chamberlain at the door.

'There are visitors from the recreation camp along the peninsula—the camp director with two boys. They have no appointment but were hoping to speak with you.' His disapproval was clear. 'I told them it was most irregular to request an audience but he was very persistent.'

Cat's gaze slewed to his. Alex could hear her thoughts as if she'd spoken aloud. The boys they'd rescued had been from the camp.

'Please show them in.'

Cat turned to Lady Enide, her tone matter of fact as she explained about the incident a few days previously. Alex noted she avoided mentioning her own part in the rescue, making it sound as if she'd been merely a bystander. Buttering him up? Or not interested in the limelight? In the circumstances he found the latter hard to believe.

Minutes later the trio were introduced and seated stiffly. Sure enough, Alex recognised the boys they'd rescued. One, good-looking and well-groomed, who'd been briefly unconscious, sat taking everything in with a mix of awe and excitement. The other, a smaller teen with baggy clothes and dark hair spilling over his face, looked surly.

'It was good of you to see us,' the camp director, Monsieur Vincenti said. 'I believe it important the boys apologise in person. Especially since the camp is funded by your personal generosity, Your Highness.' The smile he gave Cat was eager and admiring. So admiring Alex knew a sudden, unreasonable urge to send the guy on his way.

That dog-in-the-manger jealousy took Alex by surprise. He stiffened, appalled. Hadn't he washed his hands of the woman? Yet here he was, annoyed that some smarmy, yes, definitely smarmy bureaucrat toadied to her.

He was so caught up in his thoughts he barely heard the boys apologise for trespass and the trouble they'd caused. But he noticed the triumphant sideways glance the taller boy gave the dark-haired one.

'I was wary of accepting him at the camp, since he's caused trouble before, but our remit is to be accessible to all.' The camp director pursed his lips. 'Again, I can only apologise. Please be assured he won't have a chance to lead anyone else astray. I've decided to send him home.'

The slouching boy reacted to that. An abrupt stiffening, a widening of his eyes before he bent his head even lower, hiding his expression.

Instinct—the instinct of someone whose own home life had been a sore trial, despite the public façade his parents fabricated—told Alex the kid was horrified at the idea of going home.

Cat saw it too. She shifted in her seat, leaning forward.

'How do you know he's the one doing the leading astray?' Both kids stiffened at Alex's tone.

'Thomas came to us with a reputation, Your Majesty. For fighting and insubordination.' The director puffed himself up. 'It's obvious that—'

'It's not obvious at all.' Alex shouldn't have enjoyed cutting the guy off. But his pomposity and his fawning on Cat annoyed him.

'Tell me—' he turned to the bigger of the boys, the neat, good-looking one '—can you swim?'

'Yes, sir.' The kid darted a look at the man beside him and sat straighter. 'I'm fastest in my school at the hundred metres.'

'And you, Thomas? Can you swim?'

Thomas shrugged.

'Come on, boy,' the camp director scolded. 'You've been asked a question.'

'It's all right, Monsieur Vincenti. We know the answer. When the Princess and I found Thomas he was floundering to keep afloat. Clearly he can't swim.' Alex pinned the director with his gaze. 'I find it unlikely a boy who can't even keep himself afloat would dare or bully someone else into stealing a canoe and paddling it around the headland, don't you?'

For the first time Thomas lifted his head, his eyes meeting Alex's in a swift stare of astonishment, before looking away.

Cat swung round in her seat, eyes wide. 'I hadn't thought of that.' Her voice was husky with dismay. 'I should have realised.' She frowned, her teeth catching her bottom lip.

'Your Highness—' Vincenti spread his hands '—I'm sure there's a reasonable explan—'

'There's nothing at all reasonable, *monsieur*, in hosting children at a seaside camp and not ensuring they can swim.' Cat shot to her feet, rigid with outrage.

Vincenti stumbled out of his chair to stand before her, dismay on his smooth features.

'Tell me, *monsieur*,' she continued. 'Have you checked if there are any other children at camp who can't swim?'

'No, Your Highness. Our policy—'

'Your policy needs to change immediately. I will not fund an institution that puts the lives of children in danger.'

The man blanched but Alex hardly noticed. All

his attention was on Cat, taut and sparking with indignation. This was no charade. She was furious yet totally in control of herself and the situation. She intrigued him.

'You will take instant steps to assess who at the camp can swim, and to ensure all future attendees are safe in the water.'

'Immediately, Your Highness. I'll personally ensure that only those who can swim are invited.'

'And leave out those children who haven't had the luxury of swimming classes?' She shook her head and the light caught the golden tones of her hair. 'I expect you to introduce swimming classes as a priority.'

'Of course, Your Highness.' Vincenti clasped his hands. 'Though at the moment we don't have a qualified swimming instructor...'

'You run a recreation camp on the coast and you don't have a swimming instructor?' There was no missing the blaze of outrage in her fine eyes. Energy radiated from her. Even the sullen Thomas lifted his head to watch.

Cat paced to the window then back and with each step Monsieur Vincenti's consternation grew.

'I have grave concerns about the way your establishment is run, *monsieur*.' She looked so stern, so unconsciously haughty Alex found it hard to believe she wasn't the Princess she pretended to be. His curiosity intensified, and his admiration.

Technically this was none of her business. All she had to do was receive the apologies, smile at the director and send him away. Instead, she was taking responsibility as if she *were* Princess Amelie. But this was no stunt for his benefit. Alex guessed she'd all but forgotten his presence.

'An immediate review is required. I'll report my concerns to...'

'To the Board of Governors.' Lady Enide sat forward. 'I'll take care of it on your behalf today, Your Highness.'

A look passed between the two women—one he couldn't read, but there was definitely understanding there. 'Thank you, Lady Enide.'

Cat swung back to the director. 'Your first priority, *monsieur*, is to identify who else in the camp isn't safe in the water, and hire an appropriate teacher for them. In the meantime, I expect Thomas here at eight tomorrow morning, with any other children needing instruction. There will be a qualified instructor here to tutor them till you fill the post.'

She cut across Monsieur Vincenti's response and turned to the boys.

'Thomas?'

The kid met her eyes, his face expressionless.

'Do you want to stay at camp? Or would you rather go home?'

'Camp.' He mumbled the word, the sound almost drowned by Vincenti's demand that he stand.

Cat ignored the man and concentrated on the boy. 'I'll see you tomorrow. In the meantime, stay away from the water. Understood?'

Thomas nodded. His gaze was fixed on the vibrant, beautiful woman before him as if he couldn't look away.

Alex knew the feeling.

CHAPTER EIGHT

'THANK YOU FOR speaking up back there.' Cat kept her eyes on the driver beyond the glass partition as the limo slid through the palace gates and turned towards the city. 'I can't believe I didn't pick up on the relevance of Thomas not being able to swim.'

'I didn't either.' As ever, Alex's deep voice stirred wanting deep inside. Cat fought to stifle it. 'We had other things on our minds.'

Like the instant burn of desire.

Lust. Call a spade a spade. It was lust and it would burn itself out quickly.

Just not quickly enough.

Despite everything, Cat still experienced that trembling hyper-awareness when he was near. The way he'd dealt with Monsieur Vincenti and uncovered the truth about the boys had only increased her respect. It would be easier if she could detest him for his privileged life and über-confident demeanour. Or not care what he thought of her.

But he worked hard for his people and, as for

his deceptively lazy air of being able to meet any challenge—that wasn't a front. Without his formidable strength in boosting the boys to safety over that upturned canoe, Cat suspected one of them would have drowned.

Alex was competent, sexy and honest. No wonder she was attracted!

Yet he viewed her with complete contempt.

Or did he?

'Why did you want me to come with you to this meeting?' Was this a little thawing?

'I didn't.' His voice was clipped and a sideways glance revealed a set profile, jaw tight above that beautifully tailored jacket and silk tie. 'I presented a list of the places I wished to visit. I didn't know I'd have the pleasure of your company.'

So she was attending for appearances. Because it would be natural for Princess Amelie to accompany her suitor occasionally. The PM must be sweating, hoping she was up to the charade at such close quarters with Alex.

Cat's shoulders pressed back into the upholstery but she didn't let disappointment show. She was used to being the outsider, the one hiding pain. Yet she was surprised how much Alex's dismissive tone hurt.

She turned to survey the city. She'd only been here once before, the day she'd travelled to the capital for the sole purpose of leaving and never returning. Dully, she noted the pretty pastel-coloured buildings with their terracotta tiles and wrought iron balconies, the bright flowers spilling from window boxes. And beyond them the glinting sea.

But Cat couldn't summon excitement. Not with regret plaguing her. Was it stupid to wonder if, in different circumstances, she and Alex might have—?

No! He was a king. She was a commoner. Not just any commoner, but the illegitimate daughter of a king. The scandal if anyone found out would be appalling.

She was well past the age of believing in fairy tales. Her stepfather had ensured she lived in the real world, not a fantasy one, the day he'd first back-handed her for standing between him and her mother.

'This laboratory, why are you going there?'

He didn't turn his head. 'Because I'm interested.'

Cat refused to react to his dismissive tone. She'd hoped for some hint about what the place researched. The visit had been sprung on her so suddenly she'd had no time to prepare.

The professional in her hated that. Preparation was the key to maintaining control. Worse, the thought of visiting a scientific laboratory evoked memories of her struggles at school, leaving a sour metallic taste on her tongue. The taste of failure. That ancient shame.

Would it be obvious she hadn't even completed high school? That she was incapable of understanding what they were talking about? Her science teacher, a friend of her stepfather, had made it abundantly clear whenever he'd sent her from the classroom for some imagined infringement, that she hadn't the capacity to grasp the most basic concepts.

A shiver scudded across her skin. She had an awful feeling she was about to make an utter fool of herself.

Wouldn't His Majesty enjoy that?

'We're particularly excited about this new project.' The facility director spoke quickly, emphasising each point with enthusiastic gestures. 'I'm sure Your Highnesses will find it fascinating.'

He was right. Alex was intrigued by the possibilities nanotechnology provided, especially now he was considering establishing a similar centre in Bengaria.

Yet his attention kept straying to Cat who, for the first time since they'd met, looked awkward. It struck him that she was an intensely physical person. There was her uninhibited sexual passion—making love with her whole body and that fierce focus, so a night with her had felt like a life-altering experience. Plus the way she moved. She had an easy grace, a command over her body he recognised from the elite athletes he'd known.

Yet now she looked ill, not poised but cramped, her skin paler than he remembered against the purple-blue of her dress. Her eyes were wide, fathomless green wells that flickered to his then away.

She was nervous. He felt her anxiety like a vibration in the air.

Alex frowned. Why was she nervous? All she had to do was smile and nod and ask a few questions.

Yet she'd said virtually nothing since they'd arrived. This was the woman who'd easily parried Alex's earlier conversation, which he'd deliberately littered with references to people she hadn't met, to make it tough. She'd wiped the floor with that sorry excuse for a camp director to champion a kid many would write off as difficult.

'Don't you think so, Your Highness?' The director turned to Cat and Alex watched her swallow hard.

She opened her mouth, but took for ever to murmur, 'Yes, of course.'

Instead of triumphing in her discomfort, Alex found himself stepping closer, drawing the director's attention. 'I'm afraid you may have to explain the basic premise again, in words of one syllable.'

Beside him Cat stiffened. Was that sudden intake of breath indignation or because he'd hit the nail on the head? Yet she made no move to confront him or laugh off his words. What had happened to the confident woman he knew?

'My understanding of nanotechnology is virtually nothing,' Alex continued, as if he hadn't taken a special interest in the field's recent developments. 'If you could explain in lay terms it would make it much easier for me.' He turned to Cat. 'Unless that would bore you, Princess?'

'Not at all. I'm afraid I'm not…scientifically inclined either.' Cat smiled and Alex guessed he was the only one who recognised the strain in her features.

'Of course. Forgive me. I get wrapped up in my work and forget this is outside most people's understanding. Basically we're talking about science and technology at the smallest imaginable scale, so small we're viewing and controlling individual atoms and molecules.'

'It sounds…incredible,' Cat said.

The director nodded. 'I feel that way every day. Incredible but with so many possibilities. Work has been done on developing particles that will attract toxic metals found in water after an oil spill, so they can be removed more easily. And on combating water-borne bacteria.'

'That's what you're looking at here?' Cat's interest was caught. It was there in her voice as she leaned closer.

'Our research is a little different.' The scientist invited them to follow. This time Cat didn't hang back.

By the time they finished Alex had acquired the insight he needed to make a better decision about a similar lab in his own country.

Even more interesting, he'd seen Cat transform from nervous to enthusiastic. What had she been afraid of? All he could put it down to was discomfort at being out of her depth in the lab. As if anyone expected her to be an expert!

Yet her anxiety had been real. He'd felt it like an electric charge arcing from her body and it had made him feel...bad. He'd wanted to protect her.

Crazy for a guy who'd been duped by her.

He watched her shake hands with the staff. Cat had won them over. She was a natural at the meet and greet.

That didn't come easily to many royals. His father had been abysmal at it. Perhaps because in person people sensed he wasn't trustworthy. But Cat had an openness—

What was he thinking? Cat had lied straight-faced. She couldn't be trusted.

Still he had to admit she had a way with people. Not just here but at those dinners they'd shared. He'd seen guests light up when she turned her attention on them. Even Thomas, the brooding kid who looked like he'd turned teenage rebellion into an art, had responded.

This visit proved something else, he realised as they headed to the limo. The staff were St Gallans. They knew Princess Amelie from years of media reports and possibly even personal sightings. Yet they accepted Cat without question.

Alex had decided he'd fallen for this scam charade because he'd never met the Princess or taken
a particular interest in the St Gallan royal family.
For most of his life his focus had been on building his career in aeronautics. He'd never imagined
he'd one day be forced to accept the throne.

Clearly Cat was enough like Amelie to fool the
public. It wasn't just the blonde hair and stunning
eye colour. That could be achieved with dye and
coloured contacts. The similarity between them
was bone-deep. Beyond the boundary fence the
press vied for photos. Yet there was no frantic jos-
tling as if they suspected Cat was an imposter.

Who *was* this woman, settling so sedately on the
limo's back seat?

Alex's gaze lingered on the inviting curve of her
calves and the way her dress rode high for a moment, showing toned thighs. Thighs that last night
had encircled him as he'd powered into her, losing
himself in bliss. Fire raced through him, drying
his mouth and igniting need in his belly.

He yanked his eyes to the closed window between them and the driver. Alex shifted, willing
away the hardening of his groin.

Better to concentrate on the puzzle she presented.
Anything to distract from memories of how good

it had felt when she'd taken him inside her body. Or the trace of sweet, fruity perfume making his nostrils twitch.

Why did she look so like the Princess? Surely there was a family connection. A cousin?

That had to be the answer, though it surprised him Amelie's cousin worked in the US as a bodyguard. On the other hand, hadn't he lived there too, carving out a career while his cousin then his own father sat on the throne?

But even a cousin of the ruling family would be used to the limelight. Such royal connections brought public attention from birth.

'Why were you anxious?'

'Sorry?' She smoothed her hands down her dress. Deliberately drawing his attention, or because she was nervous?

Damn. He wished he could read her better. She'd taken him in so completely, now he second-guessed every impression of her.

'Back there.' He nodded to the building as the large car moved out into the traffic. 'When we arrived you were nervous.'

He didn't miss her swift glance at the driver, assuring herself he couldn't overhear. 'I'm not… comfortable in this role.' She kept her eyes averted.

'You could have fooled me. Last night you were comfortable enough to give yourself to an almost stranger.'

Her hissed breath filled the silence. In her lap her hands clenched, white-knuckled.

'We all make mistakes.'

A mistake because he'd uncovered the truth or for some other reason? The sex had been stunning, so it couldn't be that. Part of the magic had been *because* they were strangers with no long-term expectations.

But now that wasn't enough. Alex needed to understand her. Maybe then, when she was no longer an enigma, he could shove aside all thought of her.

'It was more than that. What was wrong back there?'

'I have a headache.' Her head was turned so he couldn't read her expression. 'I'd rather not talk.'

'You're a rotten liar, Cat.' It was the first time he'd called her that since he'd kissed her, when desire was a fever in his blood and he couldn't get enough of her. Her name in his mouth was a reminder of how wonderful they'd been together.

Of how she'd deceived him.

Yet now, without seeing her face, he knew she

lied. As if she wasn't an adept liar after all. Or because he'd finally wised up?

'You're afraid to tell me? Is this some other elaborate scam?'

Her head swung round, her eyes brilliant with fierce emotion.

'I'm not scamming. I've told you everything I know.'

'Not what happened at the laboratory.'

She swallowed, her slender throat working, but there was no change in her expression. 'It's personal. It's got nothing to do with you or…anything else.'

Alex crossed his arms and leaned back. 'I'll be the judge of that. Tell me or I'll ask your employer.'

She blinked. 'But if you ask him he'll know—'

'That I know you're a fraud.' He paused, letting that sink in. 'Then you can say goodbye to your payment. And wasn't there something about a fine for disclosure?' It wouldn't make any difference, he was sure, whether Cat had disclosed the truth or not. If Alex's assessment of Monsieur Barthe was correct, the man would show no mercy to someone who let him down.

Alex watched, fascinated, as her expression turned blank. No hint of vulnerability or anger. It was as if a mask had dropped down and cut her off from him. Instantly he thought of Thomas, the teen who so ostentatiously distanced himself.

Alex's curiosity intensified.

'I was…out of my depth,' she said finally. 'I know my way around the palace now and Enide has been drumming lessons in etiquette and deportment into me so I'm reasonably confident meeting a few people there.' She paused, leaving him to ponder how comfortable she'd feel next week at the gala to mark the anniversary of the special relationship between St Galla and Bengaria. Did she have any concept how significant that would be?

Of course she did. She'd agreed to the job.

'Go on—why were you out of your depth?'

Her mouth tightened. 'You sprang the visit on me. I didn't have time to prepare. I wasn't hired to go on tours of inspection!' Her voice rose, revealing what her closed expression hid.

'No, you were hired to fool me.' It was a guess but he knew he was right when her eyes widened. 'So, you knew all along.' Why did he feel disappointed? Because she'd claimed not to know?

'I didn't.' That slim neck lengthened as she sat straighter. 'Lady Enide told me this morning. She said the Prime Minister is determined Amelie will marry you. I was brought in because she's away doing something personal—don't ask me what because I don't know. They were afraid if she wasn't here for next week's celebration that would be the end of the match. I think they thought you'd be offended if she didn't show.'

Alex frowned. There wasn't going to be a match. Though, to be fair, he'd kept that to himself, wanting to tell Amelie in person.

Why was Barthe so set on the marriage? After Alex's father's depredations, Bengaria wasn't as rich as it had been. Nor did he and Amelie have a personal relationship to build on. Was the man like Alex's father, believing royals could only marry royals?

'I still want to know what happened at the laboratory. What was wrong. If you can chat with diplomats, listening to a couple of scientists shouldn't faze you.'

Silence stretched then, abruptly, she slumped as if the energy drawing her tight had switched off. She sagged against the seat, her gaze shifting to the houses on the outskirts of the city.

'*I* was wrong.' Her hands twisted in her lap. 'It was silly of me, a hangover from when I was a kid.'

Alex waited, shifting his gaze from her restless hands to her face before he was tempted to reach out and cover them.

She laughed but it didn't ring true. 'If you must know, I felt intimidated by the fact it was a science lab. I'm not academic and science was my worst subject.'

'You can't be good at everything.' Alex had always loved science but history had sent him to sleep.

Cat's mouth twisted down. 'I wasn't good at anything at school. Except getting detention.'

Alex digested that. It didn't gel with what he knew of Cat. She'd learned a lot in the time she'd been here. She couldn't have done that unless she was clever and focused.

'Are you dyslexic?'

This time the curl of her lips was almost a smile. 'Looking for excuses for me?' She shook her head. 'No, I'm not. School and I weren't a good match. My science teacher gave up even trying to teach me and I left school as soon as I could.'

'Sounds like you had a poor teacher.'

Eyes bright as gems locked onto his and he felt again that hit of sensation. 'Don't try to make excuses. The fact is I couldn't hack it.' Her jaw angled up the tiniest fraction, defying sympathy. It struck him as an interesting attitude from the woman who'd championed Thomas.

'Did you understand what you were told about the lab today? Or were you pretending?'

'I understood. I thought it was interesting. But that's different. I didn't have to learn it.'

Alex was bemused by her attitude. 'It's not different. If you could understand complex scientific principles today you could cope with high school science—in the right environment.'

For a second longer she held his eyes, then looked away towards the glimpses of sea visible through her window. 'I doubt it. And it doesn't matter now.'

Clearly it did, but there were other things he wanted to know.

'Tell me, how is it you and Amelie look so similar? Are you cousins?'

If she'd been tense before, it was nothing to her reaction now. She was so rigid she didn't even appear to breathe. Her only sign of animation was the fierce flick of a pulse below her jaw.

'Sheer coincidence.'

'As if. Come on, Cat. The truth.'

Slowly she turned and met his eyes. That blank mask was back. But more, there was a change in her eyes, as if someone had doused the inner fire he'd always seen there. For the second time in minutes he felt the compulsion to comfort her.

But who would he be comforting? He didn't know this woman. No matter how they'd shared themselves, how close to her he'd felt. He didn't know what was real and what was sham.

'I'm not the Princess's cousin. If you stay here long you'll see quite a few people with similar colouring.'

But that didn't explain the uncanny resemblance.

'If you're not related, how did they find you for this job?'

'Lambis Evangelos. He runs a multinational security firm—one of the best in the world. We met last year and he took an interest. He offered me a job if I wanted one but I was happy where I was. Apparently—' she paused and her breasts lifted as she breathed deep '—he noticed a superficial similarity to the Princess and passed on my details in case she ever needed a body double.'

Superficial similarity! Did she think he'd buy that?

'Where's your family? In America?' If her siblings were there it would explain her move across the Atlantic.

'I don't have family.' She caught his eye as he opened his mouth. 'None at all.'

Her tone was so final, her gaze so direct, he was tempted to believe her. Except he'd seen the shadow of something else in that defiant stare.

'Tell me about your parents, then. Who were they?'

For a second he thought she wouldn't respond.

'Mathieu and Catherine Dubois. He was a baker. A big man, with hands the size of dinner plates. She was much smaller, more…delicate. She ran the bakery, in a small town in the north of the country.'

'And why—?'

'That's enough!' The words fired from her, over-loud and husky with emotion. 'They're dead and I don't want to talk about them. My family is none of your business.'

So her family was the key to understanding the real Cat Dubois. That was clear. Yet instead of pressing her he held back, because the expression shadowing her features now was pain.

'You're uncomfortable.'

'Not uncomfortable, tired of your probing. You have no right…'

She stopped when he raised one interrogative eyebrow. Understanding pulsed between them.

They both knew he had a right to the truth about who she was.

It had been like this from the first—an understanding that leapt, lightning-quick between them, often without the need for words. That was why her deceit had taken him by surprise. He'd felt as if he *knew* her.

CHAPTER NINE

'YOU KNOW WHAT makes *me* uncomfortable, Ms Cat Dubois?' That indigo gaze raked her. She felt the abrasion on her skin and deeper, down where her secrets were buried.

She shook her head. In the confines of the car the air thickened and her throat dried. She couldn't have found her voice if she'd tried. Never had anyone got so close to her—not physically but crowding her very being, beating at the trapdoor she'd used to cover her past, with its disillusionment and hard-won lessons.

Cat swallowed, hating this choking feeling.

Alex leaned nearer. She could make out the thick black lashes framing his eyes, the minuscule scar on his temple, the hint of a shadow darkening his sculpted jaw.

'Deception.' His nostrils flared and she wondered if he inhaled her fragrance just as the scent of citrus and warm male skin invaded her senses. 'I loathe deception.'

Guilt spidered through her. But what more could she do? She'd apologised. She'd told him every-thing she knew about the reason she'd been hired.

'And I loathe bullying.' She told herself that's what he was doing, looming over her, trying to intimidate her into spilling the story of her past.

Except she wasn't scared of Alex. She hated that he saw her as an enemy and a liar. She hated the disappointment in his eyes, but he didn't frighten her. Staring into his hard-chiselled features, it was wanting she felt, not fear.

That realisation gave her strength to turn away, severing the connection between them. She felt the tension snap and ease and drew a deep breath, try-ing to focus on the city streets beyond the window. But she didn't feel better. How could she, when he thought her a cheat?

'Why?'

'Sorry?' She stared dully at the back of the chauffeur's head through the glass partition.

'Why do you loathe bullying?'

Cat shook her head. 'The usual.' She refused to give him chapter and verse on her early years.

'You were bullied?'

Was that regret in his tone? Surely not. Even if it was, it was far too late to make a difference.

'It was a long time ago. I learned from it.' Learned to defend herself and be strong. It had been that or live down to everyone's expectations and she'd refused to give them the satisfaction. 'I can stand up for myself now.'

'Is that why you became a bodyguard? Why you chose to make a profession of protecting people?'

The question sliced through her indignation.

'I'd never thought of that before.' It was like a light going off in her head, illuminating part of her she'd never recognised. One of the things that gave her satisfaction was knowing her clients were protected from physical harm in a way she hadn't been.

How could Alex, who'd known her such a short time, see that when she hadn't? It made her feel naked. As if he'd stepped inside the defensive walls she'd spent years building, seeing her as no one else did.

'You've got it wrong.' Though he was partly right. 'I was good at self-defence. Very good.' The free community martial arts classes had been her saviour. 'I dropped out of school with no qualifications. Fitness and martial arts skills were all I had. I fell into personal protection.'

Cat didn't mention the years of hard work, the

gruelling training and the sheer determination that
had driven her to the top of her field—an elite professional trusted with some of the world's most
well-known VIPs.

'Why do you hate deception?' she asked before
he could dig further.

'Because of my father.'

His candour surprised her, especially as he'd
been so concerned for his mother's privacy. Maybe
he finally believed she wouldn't blab to the press.
Or perhaps, given his grim expression, he didn't
care about protecting his father's memory.

Cat couldn't tear her gaze from him, even when
they passed a square and the sound of music in-
truded. She'd been curious about the capital where
her royal relatives lived, the places they knew so
well and the lives they led. But Alex was more
fascinating.

'Your father? King Cyrill?'

'The one and only.' Alex sat back and instantly
the tension thrumming between them eased. But,
as she watched the crooked line of his mouth, Cat
saw he wasn't relaxed.

'You didn't like him.'

Alex shook his head. 'My father was an unprincipled liar.' His mouth tipped up into a grim smile as he saw her surprise.

'He was greedy for power and recognition. For wealth too. He hated that he was the younger son and that the throne passed to his older brother's son, Stefan, before him. My father was Stefan's Regent for years, and every one of those years he schemed and cheated to accumulate as much power and wealth as he could from what rightly belonged to my cousin and the nation. I've been working for years to put right some of the damage but it's a long haul.'

Alex tugged at his neatly knotted silk tie, pulling it askew so he could flip open the top couple of buttons on his shirt. There was a restless energy in his movements that spoke of strong emotion. 'Shocked? You thought kings were above that kind of behaviour?'

'Not shocked at all.' Cat thought of her father seducing her mother, a palace maid, just after his honeymoon. 'I'm not awed by royalty.'

'So I gathered.' Alex's mouth turned up in a tight smile that made her heart kick. Or maybe it was the sudden heat in his eyes that reminded her of things she was trying to forget, like the feel of his arms around her, their hearts hammering as he made slow, devastating love to her.

'My father was a cold-hearted bastard.' Alex's words interrupted her reverie. 'He married for money and didn't care about his wife or son but insisted we put on a show of being a happy family. He's the reason I left Bengaria to study then found myself a job in the States. I couldn't bear the sight of him. Or the smarmy way he pretended to be a careful regent while all the time he was taking backhanders. He even—'

'Yes?'

But Alex seemed to gather himself. 'He was utterly two-faced. Living with him gave me a distaste for deception. I don't like being conned and no one fools me more than once. When my trust is betrayed that's the end.'

Yet that didn't stop him thinking about Cat. About the contrast between the laughing, confident woman he'd first met and the one petrified by the idea of talking to a few guys in lab coats.

She'd lied to him, something he abhorred, but he had to admit the Prime Minister had left her in a no-win situation. If what she'd said was true...

Alex lengthened his stride as he jogged back up the coastal track from his morning run.

What did he know of her? She and Lady Enide seemed to have developed an understanding. He respected Enide's acuity. And it seemed she, in turn, respected Cat.

What else? Cat had a strong protective streak. Look at her career choice and the way she'd championed Thomas, a kid who on the face of it was a teenage troublemaker. Except Cat, like he, had been quick to guess there was more to the boy. The way she'd faced down that pompous camp official had been magic. She'd left him with no option but to give in to her scheme for the boy.

Alex glanced at his watch. Nine. Had the swimming class finished? Would Cat be there?

He turned towards the pool. He was curious about Thomas. But if Cat happened to be there…

He'd spent another evening watching her across a polished dining table. In sea-green silk and with her hair swept high she'd looked every inch the regal Princess. Yet he'd wanted to plough his hands into her smooth wheat-blonde hair and tug it free till it rippled in waves down her back. Wanted it with a quiet savagery that had stunned him. As had the hard need pulsing through his lower body as he'd watched her smile and chat to the man beside her.

Alex had wanted her mouth on his, her hands not on the heavy silverware but on *him*.

His brain told him to wash his hands of her. She'd made a fool of him. But instinct or hormones, *something*, refused to let him ignore her.

He stopped, drawing a hand over his face. He needed a long shower, preferably ice-cold.

'That's it. Like that.' Cat's voice, soft yet enthusiastic, came from beyond the hedge around the pool. 'Hey, good work! I bet you didn't think you could do that.'

Suddenly the idea of a cold shower and a few hours preparing for his industry visits held no allure. Business could wait. After all, hadn't he originally slated this week as a long-overdue vacation?

He entered the pool yard and came to a stop under a vine-shadowed pergola. Thomas floated, arms wide, on his back at the shallow end of the pool. Metres away two little girls, arms outstretched to hold body boards, propelled themselves across the water with enthusiastic kicks.

Standing in the pool with them, wearing an encouraging smile and a familiar black bikini, was Cat, her wet hair the colour of dark honey.

Alex's pulse revved as he watched her high breasts jiggle and the water lap around the stream-lined curve of her hips. He had instant recall of how her slick skin had felt when he'd grabbed her hips in this pool and hauled her close. How she'd tasted as she all but climbed up him, as eager for him as he was for her.

This couldn't go on.

Instead of fighting Cat, using her deception as a reason to maintain his distance, he had to face the fact this gut-deep attraction wasn't dead. Wouldn't be dead till...

What?

He had no idea.

Every cell in his body screamed that he wanted this woman. Anger, and disgust at his own gullibil-ity, had made him despise her as a liar. But things weren't so simple. Cat wasn't so easily pegged.

If he looked past his damaged pride he saw a woman more complex than he'd imagined. Not complex like his conniving, self-centred father whose crocodile smiles and smarmy charm had hidden soul-deep corruption. Complex in ways that intrigued and, yes, attracted. There was real cour-age and grace in this woman, a woman who cared for a stray kid yet fiercely hid her own fears, that tugged at something deep-seated in Alex.

He crossed his arms and leaned back against a pillar. There was time before his next business meeting. He'd spend it adding to his store of knowledge about Cat.

'That's brilliant, girls.' Cat smiled. 'You're naturals. Now, get changed in the pool house. The car will be waiting for you.'

'But we can come tomorrow, can't we?'

'Absolutely.' She grinned. 'Off you go. And tell the driver Thomas will return a little later.'

'Don't tell me,' Thomas said, his voice stiff with challenge. 'I've got detention.'

Cat saw the teen on his feet, scowling. His clenched fists and hunched shoulders spoke of aggression but also—was she right?—an attempt not to show disappointment. He hadn't quite been able to hide his enjoyment of the session. Not from her. At his age she'd perfected the art of sullen posturing and studied indifference.

She ignored the hint of menace in his stance.

'There's no detention here, Thomas. Besides, you did far better than I expected from a first-time swimmer. You floated for over ten minutes without once reaching for the side. That's some achievement.'

Instead of gushing over him, Cat turned to collect the body boards. From the corner of her eye she caught a ripple of emotion on the boy's face.

Her throat tightened. Was he so unused to praise?

'Thanks for lending a hand with the girls. They wouldn't have done half as well if you hadn't showed them there was nothing to be scared of.' Cat paused. 'They trust you.'

He shrugged. 'They know me. We live in the same place.'

'The same town?' Cat stacked the boards on the side of the pool then hauled herself out, deliberately casual.

'Yeah. And the same orphanage.' That confirmed what she'd suspected from a few things the girls had said. Cat heard the challenge in his tone, the expectation of a reaction. Was he disappointed when she didn't give one?

'That explains it. They know you won't hurt them.' She turned and caught his grim expression as he climbed from the pool. Too grim for a boy his age. But she knew he'd reject sympathy. Even though the bruises on his ribs and back told their own story.

Were they from the camp or earlier? Either way, with Enide's help, and with the power that came from pretending to be Amelie, she'd make sure whoever was responsible wouldn't get another chance. Enide had backed her up when she'd confronted the camp administrator. She'd back her up in this too.

'Of course I'd never hurt them!' Outrage tightened his voice.

Cat nodded. Thomas might have a reputation for being difficult but the younger girls liked him. Which meant he wasn't violent. Who'd beaten him? Another teenager, or an adult? Anger prickled her skin.

As soon as he left she'd take steps to uncover the truth and ensure the kids at the orphanage and the camp were safe. There'd be no more beatings. But she could do more.

'They obviously look up to you. I bet you protect them when you can.'

Again that shrug.

'It must be tough though.'

'Why?' He looked suspicious, as if she'd tried to catch him out.

'Well, you're like me—a bit on the small side. Sometimes people think that means you're weak.'

'As if! I can protect myself.'

Cat met his eyes. 'Can you? How well?' She didn't let her gaze stray to the bruises fading on his ribs but they both knew she'd seen them. 'Have you learned self-defence?'

He stiffened. 'I don't need—'

'Of course you do.' Cat planted her hands on her hips. 'Everyone should know how to defend themselves.'

'I can manage.' His lower lip jutted.

'You could manage better. Not just for yourself but for the younger kids.'

'What do you think I am, some unpaid body-guard?' Yet, despite his offhand tone, Cat saw the spark in his eyes.

'Well, if you're not interested...' She picked up a towel and headed to the pool house. She'd reached the steps when finally he spoke.

'Wait. Would you...? Are you serious?'

'Of course. I could teach you—'

The sight of a long, lean figure approaching from the far end of the pool stopped her words.

What was Alex doing here?

In sweat pants and a black T-shirt that empha-sised his long-legged stride and straight shoulders, with his hair ruffled and his unshaved jaw deliciously dark, he reminded her of a pirate, stepping ashore for a bit of swashbuckling R and R.

Cat stared, aghast at her wayward imagination. An imagination that envisaged her plastered to that hard chest, offering herself for his pleasure.

Her heart hammered even harder when he met her eyes and his mouth curled in a smile. She'd missed that smile, despite its devastating effect on her internal organs. Surely something vital inside was melting?

'Taking the class yourself, then?'

'It seemed easiest.' Was that breathy voice hers? She sounded like a swooning teenager, not the competent woman people turned to in a crisis.

'How was the swimming, Thomas? Good?'

The boy nodded, his expression wary.

Damn. He'd been about to ask her to teach him and now with Alex here he'd retreat again behind the walls of his teenage pride.

Cat couldn't help every troubled teen. But she could no more turn away from this bruised boy than fly.

Alex's drawl cut off her thoughts. 'Did I hear you offer to give instruction in self-defence?'

Cat blinked. She read a gleam of intent in Alex's

expression. A gleam at odds with his laid-back demeanour.

How long had he been here? Even if he'd just arrived he couldn't miss the discoloured skin on Thomas's skinny frame. Maybe that explained why he'd buried the hatchet, for now at least.

'Princess?' Alex waggled his fingers to catch her attention.

'I was indeed. Are you interested?'

'I'm always interested.' His baritone drawl ignited that spark in her belly she'd been trying to ignore. The spark that reminded her how she'd gone up in flames and glory all through that long night with him.

Alex turned to the boy. 'But I'm not sure she's up to teaching us defensive moves. What do you say, Thomas? She's a bit on the puny side.'

Cat quelled a smile, sure now. Alex was playing into her scheme.

It felt good to have him on her side, however briefly. Like yesterday when he'd spoken up about Thomas being unable to swim. Her wariness crumbled. He didn't *need* to help, especially since it meant spending time with *her.*

'The Princess is stronger than she looks.' Thomas straightened his shoulders and lifted his chin and another layer of Cat's defensive wall eroded. No wonder the younger girls accepted the boy. He had a protective streak a mile wide, despite the chip on his shoulder.

'Thank you, Thomas.' Was that a blush on his sallow cheeks? She turned to Alex. 'Or do I have to convince you I'm up to the job?'

'I'm sure you have some moves.' His lazy smile told her he'd chosen his words deliberately. Yet she felt as if the laughter in his eyes wasn't *at* her but *with* her. 'But I'm not convinced you could handle someone my...size.'

To her amazement Cat felt heat prickle her chest and creep up her throat, making her abruptly aware she wore only a bikini. All she could think about was how it had felt to accommodate Alex's size. Remembered pleasure washed through her as she recalled the heavy thrust of his body inside hers and how he'd taken her to heaven.

Alex's eyes held hers. It was clear he remembered too. His cocky smile reminded her of the day they'd met and how much fun it had been bantering with him, underscored as it was by undeniable attraction.

Did this mean Alex had forgiven her?

No time now to find out. She grabbed her oversized T-shirt, hauling it on so it hung loose down her thighs.

Was that disappointment on Alex's face? The idea boosted her mood.

'It's not size that matters.' Deliberately she let her gaze skate low over his hard-packed body. 'It's how well you use what you've got.'

His laugh sounded choked and Cat swung back to the boy. 'I could teach you how to ward off a punch.'

'I'd rather learn how to punch back.'

Cat sympathised. It took everything she had not to let her gaze stray to his bruises.

'Anyone can start a fight,' Alex's deep voice said. 'Ending it takes far more guts.'

It sounded as if Alex spoke from personal experience. For some reason she'd imagined a member of a royal family wouldn't have to defend himself. But what did she know?

'Come on, Thomas, grab a towel and your T-shirt and we'll show you.'

'Both of you?' The kid's eyes widened. 'Really?' Of course he was stunned. A king and a princess teaching him to defend himself? Even to Cat it seemed bizarre. Living in a pastel-pink stucco palace with its own helipad and private bay was bizarre too.

But she refused to let Thomas go back till he knew how to deflect an attack long enough to call for help.

Cat led the way to some thick turf. 'I know His Highness looks a little soft—' she bit down on a smile '—but I'm hoping he's up to it.'

'Oh, I'm up to it.' That baritone drawl from just behind her made Cat's bones shiver and a pulse quicken between her legs. Alex's breath feathered her neck as he continued in a whisper for her ears alone. 'If you cast your mind back you'll remember being soft isn't a problem I have.'

Cat swallowed hard. What had begun as a bit of fun, a little banter that was heady relief after the tension of the last few days, had turned into something too dangerous.

She had no right flirting with Alex, or he with her, while he looked on her as an enemy. Especially not in front of an impressionable boy.

She stepped away and turned. Alex stood a few steps away, smiling. Thomas hung back.

'Come on, Thomas. Over near me.' Cat gestured to a spot to one side. When he was in place she beckoned to Alex. 'Now, punch me.'

Thomas stiffened in shock and even Alex frowned.

'I know you're...capable,' he said at last, 'but I'd hurt you if I connected. How about I grab you?'

She shook her head. 'We'll get to that later. Thomas, what do you notice about the way I'm standing?'

'Nothing. You're...' He paused. 'You have your feet apart and your knees a little bent.'

Cat nodded. 'And I'm watching him, looking for signs of how he's going to move. Being alert is important.'

She beckoned to Alex but, instead of throwing a punch, he lunged for her. She shifted, grabbed, turned, and was surprised that he was ready for the movement. Instead of using his momentum to toss him Cat was forced to rethink. This was a guy who could hold his own, she realised in a flurry of pleasure, her body locked against his. She twisted again and, using all her skill, upended him with merciless technique that left him lying on the grass.

'Not bad.' His mouth kicked up at one side and his eyes glinted in appreciation.

Cat stared. Many men hated being thrown by a woman. Of course Alex was taking part for Thomas's sake, but the fact he'd anticipated and parried her first move showed he'd aimed to best her. Yet still he smiled.

It wasn't fair. It would be easier if he was grumpy, like when he'd discovered her deception. When he smiled she liked him too much.

He lifted his hand and automatically she reached out to tug him up. His hand was large, the palm callused, making her recall its tender scrape on her flesh.

Cat turned away, but not before she saw Alex's smile widen. 'Now,' he said, 'you come at me.'

Cat shrugged. 'Okay.' She moved forward, half her attention on Thomas to see if he was watching. Alex's next move was unexpected, unorthodox, and ended with her on the grass, looking up into shining indigo eyes.

'You've done this before,' she gasped, refilling her lungs with a deep breath.

'I trained in martial arts.'

'Really?' She couldn't help her smile. With his dark hair flopping over his forehead and a smile teasing the corners of his sculpted mouth, he was far too gorgeous. It struck her how much she wanted him to look at her this way, not with disdain. Was his good humour all for Thomas's benefit or was it possible Alex had forgiven her? She told herself it was too much to expect.

'When did you start training?' He pulled her up.

'I was eight.'

He looked like he was about to comment but then turned away. 'How about it, Thomas? Want to try?'

Through the next hour Cat was thankful Alex was there. She taught every week back home. But he had a rapport with the boy, far easier than her own. Cat put it down partly to the fact Thomas showed an aversion to fighting a female. Plus Alex, when he put his mind to it, could be incredibly likeable.

Interesting that Thomas had no qualms about standing up to a man whose shoulders were twice as wide as his. In fact the boy was surprisingly eager. Which made Cat all the more determined to get to the bottom of those bruises.

At the end of the session he murmured goodbye and headed to the car waiting to take him to the camp.

'He's not effusive, is he?' Alex towelled his face.

'He's learned not to trust. It will take more than a morning to break down those barriers.'

'You sound like you know something about it.'

She shoved her feet into sandals. 'At home I

teach self-defence and fitness to kids. Kids you'd probably class as tough.'

'Home? You mean the States, not St Galla?'

She flicked him a glance, then had to peel her eyes away from the way his damp shirt clung to that powerful chest. Looking at him made her long for things she shouldn't. Things that were no longer possible.

'This isn't my home.'

He heard the snap in her voice. 'You weren't happy here?'

She stared across the garden towards the delightful palace, looking like some fanciful concoction in palest pink with decorative white frosting around its large arched windows and doors. Would she have been happy if she'd lived here? Was Amelie?

She wrenched her gaze away. 'I hated it. I couldn't wait to leave.'

'Because of the bullying?' Alex's quiet question slipped through her defences like a stiletto to the heart. 'Is that why you're determined to protect Thomas?'

'Someone has to care. Someone has to give him a chance.' She saw the curiosity in his eyes and hurried on. 'Thank you for this morning. You didn't have to give up your time for this.'

'Neither did you.' Something in his tone made her suddenly self-conscious.

'It's what I do. One day I plan to open a centre especially for teens. Somewhere they'll enjoy going that helps them develop their self-esteem and...' Her words petered out. She couldn't believe she was telling him this. He wouldn't be interested.

Yet when she darted another glance his way Alex's stare was thoughtful, not bored.

'Anyway, thanks again. I think Thomas opened up more, having a man to relate to.' She drew a quick breath. 'I know the last thing you want is to spend time with me—'

'That's an exaggeration.'

Her eyebrows arched. 'You don't have to spare my feelings.'

He chuckled, the sound like rich chocolate, teasing her.

She had to get out of here. Fast.

'I'm not.' His smile died and for the first time this morning he looked utterly serious. 'Despite the way you lied I find I quite...like you, Cat Dubois.'

CHAPTER TEN

I QUITE... LIKE YOU.

Cat grimaced. That wasn't what she wanted to hear from Alex. Though it was a lot better than his frosty outrage. She wanted—

'Try it again, Ms Dubois. If you manage without counting aloud that would be an improvement.'

Cat turned to Lady Enide, sitting on a chair so gilded and majestic it looked as if Louis the Sun King might have used it. Unlike Cat, wobbling on spindly heels on the polished ballroom floor, Enide looked poised, though there was a worried pleat on her pale forehead.

'I'm no good at this. You must see that.' Cat gritted her teeth, willing her desperation not to show.

'Rubbish, my girl. You're an expert in martial arts and fit enough to sprint around the peninsula every day. You have enough co-ordination to manage a waltz.'

'Not in heels and a long dress.' A borrowed ball gown of Amelie's that was loose around the bodice and dragged on the floor, a reminder that her royal half-sister was taller and better endowed. No doubt she waltzed perfectly too.

'You're making excuses. You've set your mind against this because you're scared.'

'Scared?' Cat stared, arrested.

Enide's eyes narrowed. 'I'm no fool, my dear. I realise how different all this—' she gestured to their plush surroundings '—is from your usual life.'

Cat straightened. 'Not so. I go to posh receptions all the time. To boxes at the opera and the ballet and to billionaires' parties in penthouses and private cruisers.'

'As a bodyguard—not a guest.' Those pale eyes surveyed her with something like sympathy.

'If you're suggesting I secretly yearn for a life of luxury you're wrong.' She'd worked hard for everything she had and could hold her head up in any company.

'I simply meant it must be difficult to be thrust out of the shadows and into the limelight. Into *Amelie's* life.'

'No one ever took the time to teach me to dance, but I got by.' And she didn't care. Really, she didn't. Being a tomboy, without the pretty dresses, make-up and nail polish had been no hardship. From her teens she'd tried to be as different as possible from the graceful, beautiful half-sister who appeared regularly in press reports.

She hadn't needed or wanted sleepovers with the other girls, or gossipy sessions about boys and fashion that she'd never been invited to join anyway.

Cat turned and saw her reflection in one of the mirrors. She'd never owned a pink dress. Her hand splayed over the deep carnation pink folds. Wearing this gown with its strapless, glittery bodice and cinched-in waist she looked like a stranger.

'Every girl should learn to waltz,' Enide said crisply. 'There's nothing like being whirled around the ballroom by the right man, a man with strong hands and the devil in his eyes, to make a woman feel...all woman.'

Cat turned to see the older woman smile reminiscently.

'Enide?'

'Don't look so shocked. I wasn't always this old.' She flapped one elegant ringed hand. 'Now, try again.'

Cat shook her head. 'It would be better to change the arrangements. It's too late to teach me to dance.

I was told a small reception.' She'd said it before but it had made no difference. She'd been deliberately misled about this job—a job she couldn't wriggle out of. Cat felt caught in a vice—pressure from the Prime Minister, from Alex, from the need not to let Amelie down the only time her sister needed her.

Enide sighed. 'If I could, I would. But any change now would cause talk and that's what we're trying to avoid. I blame myself for not checking you could waltz.'

'But if I have to dance with lots of people someone will realise I'm not Amelie. You must see that!'

She was tempted to blurt out that Alex already knew the truth, but she couldn't risk the penalty clause in her contract, or the threat of being blacklisted.

Enide nodded, her mouth turning down. 'I agree. However, it's not as bad as you think. Open the dancing with King Alex. One waltz only, then retire to watch. You'll have done your duty. Everyone will understand that, so soon after the tragedy in your family, you're not ready for a night of dancing.'

Cat opened her mouth to object, then clapped it shut. That fragile look was back on the older woman's face. Clearly she was deeply affected by the deaths of Amelie's brother and his wife. Clearly too, she had no more enthusiasm for this royal reception than Cat.

Every demand placed on her came from the PM. Enide was doing her best to ensure that Cat and Amelie didn't come unstuck.

Cat could only try to fill her half-sister's shoes and hope no one noticed Cinderella had two left feet.

Alex strode into the palace, his mind on his meeting. He wouldn't do business with the company he'd visited. He didn't like its ethics. But the real reason he'd cut the meeting short was the issues he had to sort out here.

His pace slowed as music reached him. Waltz music. Curious, he turned from the curving marble staircase and followed the sound to a pair of large doors, slightly ajar.

He'd been right. The *Emperor Waltz*—his mother's favourite. Alex remembered seeing her years ago, swirling around the dance floor in some VIP's arms. She'd been graceful, gorgeous and more animated than he'd ever seen her with his father. She loved dancing, but Cyrill had never partnered her.

He'd never spent time with his wife. He was always too busy working on his next shady deal.

Curious, Alex pushed one of the doors wide. Golden, late afternoon light slanted in, gleaming on the polished floor and spotlighting the woman dipping and twirling, arms raised as if resting on an invisible partner. There was no one else in the room.

Her hair was up in one of those oh-so-neat bun arrangements that he'd detested ever since he'd seen her gorgeous locks rippling across her bare shoulders. She wore a grimace and a ball gown that displayed enough flesh to send lust quaking through him.

For days he'd been with her each morning while she taught Thomas self-defence. Each evening he spent with her and Enide and a variety of tame guests. And every day that gnawing urge grew stronger—to forget she'd duped him and relieve his burning frustration with her sweet, sexy body in his bed.

'What are you doing?' He shut the door behind him. 'Stupid question. But why dance alone?'

Cat swung round, her skirt belling around her. She was breathing hard. Alex's throat dried as he imagined tracing a line along—

She yanked the bodice of her dress up. Flags of deep rose pink painted her cheeks, almost matching the colour of her dress. Though from the fit it clearly wasn't *her* dress.

'What are you doing here?'

'I'm staying here, remember? You haven't answered. Why are you dancing alone?'

She shrugged. Alex watched those bare shoulders rise stiffly and was struck abruptly by her vulnerability.

It wasn't something he naturally associated with Cat. She could take on most comers in physical combat and she had a sharp tongue when riled. He guessed if she had any idea how he responded to that forlorn look in her fine eyes she'd be horrified.

She turned away to switch off the music, her movements quick and far more fluid than when she'd been attempting the waltz. Strange how someone so supremely active should look uncomfortable dancing.

'It turns out there will be dancing at the reception.'

'You're out of practice?'

Her laugh was humourless. 'I've never danced in my life. Now they want me to open a royal ball, with you.' Was that panic underlying her clipped words?

A frown tightened Alex's forehead. 'How can that be?'

'Because I'm taking Amelie's place, of course.'

'I mean how can you never have danced?'

Her mouth flattened. 'You sound like Lady Enide. Not everyone grows up attending balls.' With her hands on her hips she was helping gravity tug her dress lower. Alex fought to keep his eyes on her face, not those delicious curves. 'There's no need to look so smug!' Her gaze flashed fire and perversely he wanted more of that crackling energy. The alternative—seeing her looking almost lost—bothered him.

'You must have gone to some sort of dance.'

She shook her head. 'Never.'

In her ill-fitting gown, and her hair dressed in someone else's style, it struck him how hard it must be, playing Cinderella in another woman's place.

What had Cat's life been? She'd never danced. She'd been bullied and hated talking about her family. His suspicions had been roused when he'd seen her fierce determination to protect young Thomas and recalled her saying her father had hands the size of dinner plates. Surely that wasn't the first thing that should come to mind when describing a parent?

But what did he know? His father had been a slimy piece of work. Instead of using his hands, he'd cut people down to size with his tongue and made them pay in other ways for disrupting his plans.

'I'll teach you.'

Instantly she stepped back. 'There's no need.'

'You'll never master it alone.'

Predictably that chin lifted. 'Enide partnered me for a while but—'

'But you need a man.'

'I don't need...' Her voice stopped as he curled his arm around her waist and took her hand. She fitted him exactly.

'Don't argue. Put your other hand on my shoulder and follow my lead.'

'But I don't...'

'Don't argue, Cat. Or this will take even longer.' Not that he minded longer. Looking into her dazzling eyes, breathing in her scent, holding her close, was the best he'd felt since their tryst at the pool.

'You're holding me too tight.'

He shook his head. She was right but he was damned if he'd put a proper distance between them now.

'Stop twitching.'

'But it's uncomfortable. Enide insisted I wear heels and stockings. I *hate* stockings. They're even worse than pantyhose.' She was talking too fast, her breath nervous little puffs that landed on his chin.

She was right to be nervous.

Alex shut his eyes, fighting the urge to forget dancing and seduce her here, where anyone could walk in. He'd start with those stockings. A shudder ripped through him at the thought of Cat's long, toned legs in stockings. Of her smooth upper thighs above wispy nylon, then the warm silk of her—

'Alex? What's wrong?'

'Nothing.' He cleared his throat and opened his eyes. Hers looked huge and uncertain.

Did she feel the same shuddery need? And more—that too-tight feeling in the chest? He'd never known it with any other woman. Even when he'd been furious with her, he hadn't managed to conquer it.

'Thank you for volunteering to teach me,' she

said solemnly. 'And for helping Thomas. I appreciate it.'

Alex tried to smile but his mouth was too tight. Absurd how tense he was.

'It's nothing. And I haven't taught you yet.'

'I know it's asking a lot. Even now that you *quite like* me.' A hint of a smile curled her lips.

'Witch.' He rubbed his thumb over the centre of her palm in a deliberate caress that made her breath hitch and her pupils widen. He loved how receptive she was to his touch. That at least had always been real between them.

'If we're going to dance we need music.' She broke away abruptly.

Madness, sheer madness, to let him hold her like that.

But what option did she have? Her lesson with Enide had been a disaster. Somehow she had to learn the right dance moves.

The trouble was with Alex it wasn't dance moves she had in mind. Especially when he touched her that way.

What did he mean by it?

It was difficult enough when they met each morning, helping Thomas. Especially as she found herself *liking* him as he took the boy under his wing. He was a natural role model for the kid— apparently easy-going but with an inner strength that demanded respect.

Cat switched on the music. It started softly but her nerves sparked at the thought of being held in Alex's arms as he swept her around the room.

As if that was going to happen. More like she'd lame him with these spiked heels.

'Cat?'

She drew a deep breath and spun round. He opened his arms invitingly and it was the most natural, scary thing in the world to walk into them. This time he didn't hold her too close. She registered a sliver of disappointment at the distance between them. Yet the feel of his hand pressing her waist through the silk gown made her skin flush.

'First up, don't look down at your feet. You can't see them anyway in that skirt. Look at my face.'

Reluctantly Cat shifted her gaze. There was a fizz of sensation as their eyes met.

'How am I supposed to see what I'm doing if I don't look?'

'You don't. I'll look out for both of us. That's why I lead.' He paused, his mouth curling in a smile that made her heart kick. 'You have to let yourself go completely and trust me. Can you do that?'

All too easily.

That night in the pool house she'd trusted her instinct and followed blindly where he led. It had been the single most amazing experience of her life. The ease with which she'd given him her trust was terrifying.

'Come on, Cat. Take a risk.'

The music was an enticing rhythm and Alex moved. She followed, moving backward, silently counting the beats and trying to anticipate the direction of his turn.

Her knee bashed his and her foot came down on his shoe.

'Sorry.' She bit her lip, stepping back, but Alex stepped with her, pulling her nearer.

'Don't apologise. You don't let Thomas apologise when he doesn't get something first go.'

'That's different.'

'Not different at all. You're learning. Cut yourself some slack. If you relax a little you might enjoy yourself.'

Enjoy making a fool of herself in front of him? 'I doubt it. I don't have the knack.'

Another smile. This one sent flames roaring through her blood. 'Of course you do. Let me make all the moves.' He leaned closer, his voice a rumbling whisper. 'Waltzing is like making love. Didn't you know?'

Cat's eyes popped wide but before she could respond his grip firmed and the music swelled and suddenly they were moving. Not the tentative, carefully measured steps Enide had taught her, but a wheeling, whirling circle of movement that turned the rest of the room into a kaleidoscope blur.

Cat's grip tightened on Alex's broad shoulder for balance. Her long skirts belled out around her in a soft swoosh of silk. His knee and thigh pressed against hers then retreated then touched again, prompting her to move, to step and spin. It was a miracle but somehow, without actually trying, Cat was dancing.

She wasn't pressed up against his body but she was close enough to feel his breath warm on her face and inhale the scent that was his alone. She saw the pulse at his neck and the way his mouth curved and understood what he meant about the intimacy of the dance. They were fully clothed. Anyone seeing them would notice nothing untoward. Yet the way her body responded so completely to his, receiving and reacting to each tiny message about the direction of the dance…it was completely instinctive. Just, as he'd said, like sex.

Round and round they went, down the length of the ballroom and back. Cat caught glimpses of them in the mirrors over his shoulder, a blur of blush pink against sober charcoal grey. Like figures in some fairy tale—elegant and handsome.

'Look at me.' Again that deep voice. But this time the command was a growl.

Cat looked up and instantly was lost in the dark sea of his eyes.

Alex twirled her faster, the momentum threatening to spin her out of his arms, except his hold, like his gaze, was steady, keeping her with him. He was totally in command, easy but firm and precise in every movement.

For only the second time in her life Cat revelled in ceding total control. The first time had been when Alex had taken her on a trip of sensual discovery that shattered her habitual barriers, leaving her naked in a way that had little to do with her lack of clothes.

This should scare her.

Instead she was thrilled. Exultant.

The hand at her back urged her nearer to that hard-packed heat and muscle. His mouth curled in a smile that held nothing back. It shot delight right through her.

Suddenly Cat found she was laughing. Spinning and twirling as the music soared and swooped and the mirrors and windows flashed by. She felt like she was flying. She felt—

They slammed to a halt, her long dress swooshing around her legs, her heart pumping hard, her breasts pushing up against the ill-fitting bodice.

Alex released her hand, lifting his warm palm to her cheek as his arm tightened on her waist. His breath was rough, like hers, as the joy in his blazing eyes faded to something that made her gulp.

She should step away. Say how remarkable it was that she'd been able to keep up.

But the expression on his face, or perhaps the strange fluttery feeling deep within, stopped her words.

'Cat.' It was a soft breath of air. A caress. The single word in that impossibly deep register rippled through her in endless waves.

She swallowed, sought for something to say, but instead found only a yearning, melting sensation as she looked into eyes the colour of twilight.

'Beautiful Cat.' His hand slid up, fingers spearing her hair, massaging her scalp in slow, delicious caresses till the tightly secured tresses loosed and fell. She heard hairpins scatter on the floor.

'That's better.' Alex smiled and the impact made it hurt to breathe. 'Now you look like you.'

'Alex?' She planted her hand on his chest, trying to anchor herself, for his words made her knees wobble. The steady thud of his heart beneath her palm should have reassured but the intimacy of touching him made her more, not less unsure. 'I don't understand.' What had happened to his censure? His distrust?

'I can't get enough of you, Cat.'

She sucked in a shocked breath, struggling to process his words and the intent look on his face.

Despite caution, despite pride, she felt herself glow. An answering need rose within her, urgent and unstoppable.

'You don't want me! You made that clear.' Pride made her lift her chin, as if neither of them heard the tell-tale hitch in her voice. As if she was as strong as she pretended to be, when all the while her silly heart jolted against her ribcage and excitement and anxiety knotted her stomach.

'I explained and apologised but it didn't make any

difference.' She shouldn't care what he thought, or what he wanted. He'd rejected her.

Yet she did care. Despite everything, she did.

She'd discovered far more than Alex's charisma and sex appeal. He was patient but firm with Thomas, giving his time freely without being asked. With Enide he was amusing and solicitous, especially when the older woman was stressed and looking fragile beneath her armour of formidable hauteur. It had struck Cat that though he knew Enide was part of the scheme to dupe him, he treated her not as an enemy but as an old lady carrying a heavy burden of stress.

With Cat he'd been...understanding. She knew he'd asked their guide at the lab to speak simply solely for her, because he hadn't quite managed to hide his own level of knowledge. He'd pushed her to talk about her past but his response to her revelation about dropping out of school had made it seem unimportant. Then he'd opened up about his family and she'd found herself feeling that connection she'd thought severed between them. And since he'd begun helping her with Thomas's lessons she'd found herself enjoying his company, admiring him, and...

'What are you thinking?' His deep voice cut off her thoughts.

'That this is a bad idea. You need to let me go.' Because the appalling truth was Cat didn't have the power to break his gentle hold. What had Alex done to her? How had he sapped her willpower?

Slowly he shook his head. 'I can't, Cat. I've tried, ever since I realised you lied to me, but it's not working. The more I'm with you, the better I know you, the harder this is.' His words were an uncanny echo of her thoughts.

'I was angry. Too angry.' Yet he didn't look angry now. Her heart gave a single mighty thump then raced on.

'Because I deceived you.' They were back where they'd started. Despite her hurt, Cat couldn't blame him for his anger. No one liked to be made a fool of.

'It wasn't all your fault.' His words surprised her. 'I believe that you didn't know I'd be here. I followed up what you told me with some discreet digging. It turns out the Prime Minister is the one pushing the royal marriage. He's a ruthless, conniving man and he's convinced the regency shouldn't go to a single woman like Princess Amelie. He wants her married to a *suitable* man who can be a role model for the young Prince.'

As he spoke Alex combed his fingers through her hair, drawing it around her shoulders and breasts, all the while holding her gaze. It was one of the most sensual, arousing experiences of her life. Pleasure exploded across her scalp and shoulders, sending shockwaves through her, making it hard to concentrate on words.

Her tongue felt thick and clumsy but she forced herself to speak. 'That doesn't excuse what I did.'

'We all make mistakes.'

'Alex?'

His mouth tipped up in a hint of a smile and his arm tightened around her waist.

'Lying is a hot button for me. When I discovered the truth...' He shrugged. 'I held you equally to blame with those behind the charade. But what I conveniently blanked from my mind was that you hadn't set out to seduce me. I was the one seducing you. And that, whatever this is between us, it was close to irresistible.'

Alex paused, his eyes searching hers. 'It still is.'

Cat gasped, and inhaled that familiar warm, citrus tang she remembered from when she'd kissed him all over. A terrible trembling started deep inside.

'Cat? Tell me it's not just me feeling this.'

'Feeling what?' she croaked, fighting the undertow of longing that threatened to sweep her away.

His gaze was steady. 'Attraction. Desire. Respect. Liking.' His hand slid from her hair to her face, cupping her cheek; his thumb swiped the corner of her mouth and Cat struggled not to dissolve at his feet.

'Not just sex?' Her voice was unrecognisable.

'Not just sex.' His gaze pinioned her. 'I've seen who you are, Cat Dubois. I don't pretend to know everything but I like what I see. More than I'd thought possible.'

He swallowed and she saw his Adam's apple bob in that strong throat. 'I *want* what I see, despite how this started. The question is, do you still want me?'

Dazed, Cat felt herself drowning in his darkened gaze. She read heat, hunger and honesty. He liked her, he wanted her. He *respected* her. He was offering the chance to continue where they'd left off with an affair that would be short but intense and oh-so satisfying.

Cat licked dry lips, trying to find words. Instantly he zeroed in on the movement. A second later he lowered his head. But, instead of taking her mouth, he pressed a kiss to her cheek, then another on her jaw, then more, tracing her jawline and down her throat.

'It has to be your decision, Cat. I won't push you.'

No, he'd make her lose her mind with devastating kisses.

Cat inhaled deeply and was suddenly conscious of the silk bodice sagging across her breasts. Conscious she wore another woman's finery. She was in unfamiliar surroundings and out of her depth.

She told herself none of that mattered. What she felt for Alex was real, whether she wore jeans or gym gear or borrowed stilettos.

But she no longer trusted her judgement. Not when Alex—*King* Alex—made her feel things she'd never before experienced.

With a gasp of disbelief at her own actions, Cat pushed him back. Their eyes locked and she felt the compulsion to slam her mouth to his, let him sweep her into mindless delight.

Instead, with a strength she hadn't known she possessed, Cat spun away. Reefing up her billowing skirts, she stumbled to the door. She needed time to think. Time alone.

It was only as she stumbled up the wide staircase that she realised she'd left her satin shoes behind.

CHAPTER ELEVEN

CAT LEANED OVER the balustrade, looking down into the palace foyer where staff bustled, carrying massive flower arrangements and chairs, preparing for tonight's festivities. The front doors were open and two men unrolled a carpet of royal St Gallan green edged in gold.

She rubbed her hands up her arms as nerves prickled. Already her hair was up in a style that looked frighteningly regal. When she'd looked in the mirror she'd seen a stranger. How would she look after a session with the make-up artist and wearing the amazing dress, made to measure, that had been delivered?

Knowing Alex was at yet another meeting, she'd aimed to clear her head with a quick walk through the palace galleries. But she felt as muddled as before.

Yesterday Alex had held her close and told her he wanted her. That he'd forgiven her deception and more. So much more. Cat had spent last evening in her room, pleading a headache. It hadn't been much of a lie. Her head had swum and she'd felt wrung out.

His words, his expression as he'd held her, had made Cat want to surrender to her feelings for him. Feelings she hadn't been able to eradicate, even when he'd hated her.

She felt a foreigner in her own body, her own mind. Romance had been scarce in her world. But that didn't mean she was a pushover.

Yet, even as she thought it, she recalled the expression on Alex's face, the roughened timbre of his voice as he spoke about needing her. He'd said this wasn't just sex, despite the thrumming sexual attraction, and she'd been on the brink of giving him whatever he wanted.

Yet what more could they share? And if it was simply sex, was she ready for such a brief liaison? Could she walk away, heart whole afterwards? She was due to leave tomorrow. She wasn't naïve enough to imagine a king would carry on a long-distance relationship with a bodyguard. He in his palace in northern Europe and she in New York or wherever work took her.

That was without the complication of her true identity. If fairy tales happened and he did want her even then, sooner or later someone would discover her past and reveal the sordid truth for the world to devour over morning coffee.

Cat shivered at the thought. Not merely of facing her past, but of how the scandal might affect Alex and Amelie.

So, all they could offer each other was sex. A steamy liaison for a week in Bengaria if she followed Alex before she took up her next job.

She was so tempted. She told herself she was fascinated by what he'd told her of his people's fierce pride and warm hearts and how, when things looked grim, they'd pulled together. Under his leadership, Bengaria was now becoming a centre for innovation and investment.

But it wasn't Bengaria that drew her. It was Alex.

Hers was a blood-deep craving.

Cat shook her head and hurried to her room. The sooner she—

'There you are.' Enide was at her door. She looked tired but there were spots of colour high on her cheeks.

'Lady Enide. Are you all right?' This situation was so difficult. She'd been increasingly worried about Enide, despite her self-contained air.

'I have someone who needs to speak with you.'

She glanced around as if checking they were alone. Cat followed her gaze, wondering where the visitor was. She hoped it wasn't another demand from the Prime Minister. Despite the penalty if she walked away from the job, Cat was close to pulling the plug on this whole masquerade.

'Not here.' Enide opened the door to Cat's suite and ushered her in. It was only then Cat saw the slimline phone in the other woman's hand.

Enide put the phone to her own ear. 'I have her here. Are you absolutely sure—? Yes, of course. I will. But please, take care of yourself.'

Cat stared. It couldn't be the Prime Minister's office, not with Enide sounding clucky as a broody hen.

Enide straightened, putting her hand over the phone. She opened her mouth then closed it. Cat's curiosity rose. Then Enide held the phone out. Cat took it and was bemused when the older woman briefly clasped her other hand and squeezed. Then she left the room, gently closing the door behind her.

'Hello?'

'Ms Dubois?' The voice was female, warm and young. Cat relaxed a fraction.

'Yes.'

'It's Amelie here. Princess Amelie.'

Cat staggered and groped for a seat, plopping down into a velvet-covered chair near the window. She heard her blood rush in her ears, felt the quick hammer of her heart. She'd waited all her life to connect with her other family; even in the years when she'd told herself she didn't *want* any contact, the desire had still been there, hidden beneath her pride.

'Your Highness.'

'Amelie, please.' There was a pause so long Cat wondered if the line had dropped out. 'May I call you Cat?'

'Of course.'

'Thank you.' Another pause. Cat wondered at the sudden certainty Amelie was nervous too. Almost as nervous as her. But how could she possibly know that? 'Are you all right, Cat?'

'I'm sorry?' Cat pressed a hand to her forehead, confused.

'I asked if you're okay.' There was a soft sigh on the other end of the line. 'I've just found out about this scheme for you to take my place at tonight's reception. I had no idea. The event should have been cancelled when I told the Prime Minister I wouldn't be there. I believed it *had* been cancelled.' Steel underscored her words.

'I haven't been watching the news, you see, and I haven't been in regular contact with anyone at the palace so I didn't know you'd been brought in. Are you all right?'

Amelie was asking *her* if she was okay?

'I'm fine. I…well, I'm not very good at being a princess, but I'm muddling through.'

'Even with King Alex in the palace?'

Cat rubbed her hand across her brow. She was on thin ice no matter what she said.

'Cat? Are you sure you're all right?'

Cat didn't know if it was tiredness or frustration at being in such a situation, hemmed in by other people's demands. Or the totally unexpected concern in Amelie's voice. Her *sister's* voice. But suddenly she'd reached breaking point.

She dropped her hand and stared at the view beyond the window. From here she could see one end of the pool where she and Alex had made love all night long.

Her jaw tightened. She was sick of pretending.

'I'm fine. And Alex knows the truth. He guessed some time ago.'

'Yet he's still there?' Cat heard Amelie's astonishment.

'He knows it's not your doing. He blames Monsieur Barthe. But he's willing to go along with the
pretence so there's no public scandal.' She paused,
wondering how to say what needed to be said. 'But
there's something else you need to know. He made
it clear, even before he found out who I was, that
he wasn't interested in marriage.'

'Thank God. That's one thing less to worry
about.'

'You're pleased?' Cat was confused.

'I agreed to entertain the idea, but my heart
wasn't in it.' Amelie's laugh sounded bitter.

'Are *you* all right? I've been worried you might
be in trouble.'

'That's kind of you.' She sighed. 'Things haven't
gone quite as I'd expected but I'm coming home.
I'd like, very much, to meet you. I…' There was a
long pause. 'I didn't know you existed till Enide
told me.'

Cat felt a lump choke off her breathing. Amelie
knew or guessed they were half-sisters and still
she wanted to meet. It was more than Cat had ever
dared hope.

'I'd like that.'

'Good. I'm looking forward to it too.' She paused. 'Now, about tonight. I'll see if I can get there in time. Transport is a bit limited from here and—'

'It's all right. I can do it. It's only for a couple of hours and with Enide and Alex watching out for me I'll be fine.'

She would too. She could do this. Afterwards she'd leave and take up her own life again. And she'd have the prospect of meeting her sister to look forward to.

'Alex?' What had Amelie heard in her voice?

'He's been…helpful.' She opened her mouth to say he'd taught her to waltz but the memories of their dance were too personal, too intimate to share.

'I see.' Amelie paused. 'Are you absolutely sure? I couldn't guarantee I'd get there exactly on time but—'

'I'm sure. I'll manage. I'm sure you have other things on your mind than tonight's reception.' It must have been something major to take her from her kingdom. 'I hope Prince Sébastien is well.'

'He's fine.' The warmth in Amelie's voice was obvious. 'Much better than before.' A man's voice sounded in the background. 'I'm sorry. I have to go. Are you sure about tonight? I can try—'

'Absolutely.' If Amelie arrived late, missing the opening of the event, questions were sure to be asked. Better that she, Cat, play the part one last time.

'Thank you, Cat. If you can manage tonight it will give me a little time to...organise things. But we'll talk soon and arrange to meet, either in St Galla or elsewhere.'

Alex stood in the echoing foyer, smiling and greeting guests entering the palace on the carpet that stretched to the white gravel driveway. On his left stood Lady Enide in silver and pearls, and on his right was the St Gallan Prime Minister, taking the temporary role of host.

Since the royal family was still mourning the recent deaths of King Michel and his wife, the official line was that Princess Amelie wouldn't formally host the event.

It was a clever way of reducing the chances of Cat being recognised as an imposter. Alex had to admire Monsieur Barthe's deft control of a tricky situation. Except the more he saw of the man's methods, the more he disliked him. He reminded Alex of his own father—a man who'd shamelessly lied and manoeuvred situations to his own ends.

This was the man responsible for Cat's charade, for the lies Alex had been fed. He intended to ensure the man paid a high price for his devious tactics, as soon as tonight was over and Cat was safely away from here.

Cat. As he smiled and shook hands he acted on autopilot. His mind was on her.

Twice she'd run from him. That first day on his yacht when she'd dived into the sea rather than admit the attraction between them. Then yesterday when he'd told her he wanted her, cared for her.

She'd looked like a doe caught in headlights. Her eyes huge with shock. But he'd known, or thought he'd known, she felt the same. The sound of her laughter as they'd danced, the way she responded to him, the light in her eyes. He'd *felt* the connection, as strong and true as ever. It had withstood his fury and hurt pride at her deception. It made a nonsense of his intention not to get involved with anyone till he'd achieved what he needed to in Bengaria. It turned him, and his plans, upside down.

Yet she'd spent the last twenty-four hours avoiding him. Because he'd been wrong and she felt nothing? Or because she felt too much?

It *had* to be the latter.

Every instinct told him Cat was in as deep as he.

It was only that understanding that had stopped him invading her privacy to force a discussion. She needed time. She needed—

A ripple of excitement passed through the crowd. Faces turned up and those in the receiving line stopped to look.

Alex turned and his heart stalled.

She was magnificent.

Poised at the top of the staircase was a slim, breathtaking woman in a dress that looked black till she shifted and the light from the chandelier caught a gleam of darkest green. Her shoulders and arms were bare and from her hips soft folds fell to the floor. Gems glinted in her blonde hair and diamonds glittered at her throat.

It wasn't the gems or couture gown that stopped his breath. It was Cat. In baggy running shorts and an old T-shirt he wanted her. In a bikini she was sexy and enticing. But here, now, facing an evening, and a crowd, that must be utterly daunting, she was composed and elegant.

Her bravery knocked him sideways. Her determination. He'd seen her nerves yesterday and guessed enough about her past to know she was out of her depth in this environment. Yet she'd promised to do this and here she was, utterly superb.

'Excuse me.' Ignoring protocol and curious stares, he left the receiving line and cut his way through the crowd, taking the steps two at a time till he reached her.

This close he saw the fear in her eyes. When he reached out and took her hand in his it trembled, then, to his delight, squeezed back.

'You look beautiful.'

She shrugged, and her necklace, a solid circle of diamonds with pendant diamond stars, winked and flashed. 'It's the dress.'

Alex took his time scrutinising the velvet bodice, cut to accentuate her slim figure and tiny waist, and the delicate layers of lightweight fabric that made up the skirt. She shifted nervously and a sprinkle of diamonds winked from the folds.

'It's not the dress. It's you.'

He watched rosy colour cover the upper slopes of her breasts, then climb to her throat and cheeks. Her response to that simple compliment made Alex want to haul her to him and never let her go.

Face it, you always want that.

He'd given up lying to himself about it.

'Alex? What is it?'

He shook his head. This wasn't the time.

'About what you said yesterday—'

He stopped her words. 'It can wait.'

'I shouldn't have run from you.' Her chin angled in an endearingly familiar movement. 'I was… overwhelmed but it was cowardly of me.'

Staring into her stern, slightly bewildered features, Alex felt something tumble in his chest. The hubbub of voices at the bottom of the stairs faded as he read her confusion. He wanted to carry her off in his arms and leave the Prime Minister explaining *that* to the crowd below.

'You look fierce. I thought you weren't angry with me any more.'

'I'm not.' It was true. Finally he'd been able to move past his knee-jerk hatred of lies—enough to see the fix she was in and the woman she was.

He'd spent so long wondering which was the real Cat and if there even *was* a real Cat. Till he realised he'd known her all along but let himself be blinded by anger.

From that first day he'd responded to her. Cat was the delicious mermaid with the quick tongue who was so capable in a crisis and made a living protecting others. The woman who championed kids. Who made love with her whole being—body and soul. Who was scared of failure but brave enough to befriend the formidable Lady Enide.

Alex lifted her hand to his mouth and pressed his lips to her wrist. She tasted unique. No one else in the world tasted so good. He stroked his thumb over her fluttering pulse and was rewarded with a soft hitch of her breath. Her pulse was as uneven as his.

'I'm wrestling the urge to abduct you. To take you away from this crowd so we can continue yesterday's discussion. But that will have to wait till later.'

She nodded. 'When we can be private.' Her eyes blazed so bright, Alex almost abandoned his good intentions. But the murmurs from the crowd grew louder. They were attracting gossip.

'Come on, Cinderella. Time for your ball.'

To Cat's surprise, she enjoyed the evening she'd been dreading.

She was used to blending into the background, being part of the invisible machinery that made events like this tick. Facing the blaze of attention should have been difficult.

Except one look at Alex's approving face, his half smile, and Cat felt as if she could take on anything.

Alex was at her side all evening, supportive as

they mingled with the wealthy and privileged and high achievers from various fields. His ease and good humour were infectious. Or maybe it was the realisation she'd stopped fighting her feelings that made her giddy and excited.

When he'd loped up the staircase, his athletic stride somehow not at odds with his exquisitely tailored formalwear, her heart had stuttered. She'd never dreamed of Prince Charming, never needed one. But if ever a man fitted the role it was Alex of Bengaria.

With his chiselled features, glossy dark hair and wide-shouldered swimmer's body, he looked the part as no other could. But it wasn't that making her body hum. It was Alex the man. The charmer. The companion. The lover. The partner.

When he'd kissed her wrist then led her down the stairs she'd floated on air, like when he'd taught her to dance. She spent the next fifteen minutes in a blur of delight, so the challenge of entering the ballroom and facing the throng was over before she realised.

'Your Highness?'

Cat blinked and realised Alex was standing before her, proffering his hand. Behind him the richly dressed crowd had cleared space at the centre of the ballroom and from the end of the room came the sound of music. The orchestra played a familiar waltz.

Her heart knocked her ribs as she looked up into twinkling eyes.

'You trust me not to step on your feet this time?' she whispered.

He leaned in as she placed her palm in his. 'I'll brave even that for the chance to hold you.'

A laugh bubbled up. 'I knew from the first you were a smooth talker. Dangerous.'

He smiled. That private smile that was no more than a flicker of movement at one corner of his lips. Its effect was devastating, turning her insides over.

'But you don't run from danger, do you, Cinderella?'

He drew her into the centre of the room. Hundreds of eyes were fixed on them but Cat was aware only of Alex, the enticing promise in his look, and the mad yearning to enjoy what they had and forget tomorrow.

His strong arm curled around her waist, drew her close. His smile grew as she placed her hand on his shoulder. Beneath the fine tailoring he was all hot, hard muscle and bone. Cat had trained with him daily, touching him as she demonstrated defensive moves. But this was different. A thrill rippled through her as the music swelled and Alex stepped forward.

This time Cat didn't see them in the mirrors as they passed by. The crowd wasn't even a blur on the sidelines. Her eyes were locked on Alex's as they spun together, light as a leaf on the breeze. The soft layers of her skirt swished around her, the rhythm of the music becoming the beat of her blood while Alex's breath warmed her face.

Cat was euphoric. She couldn't explain it. There was nowhere she and Alex could go with this attraction except a short—far too short—affair. But her heart, her very essence screamed that this magic couldn't be ignored.

She spun and dipped and swayed in Alex's arms, more alive than she'd ever been.

It was crazy. She'd regret it. But she could no longer deny the *rightness* of being with him.

Alex swung them to a halt and Cat realised the music had ended. Her breathing was heavy, the diamonds rising and falling at her breast. Still he didn't look away. The flare of approval in his eyes should have singed her. Instead she felt exultation burst like sunshine in her veins.

Cat leaned in so only he could hear. 'You're right, Your Highness. I've given up running.'

CHAPTER TWELVE

CAT TIGHTENED HER robe then rapped on Alex's door.

Downstairs, staff still tidied up after the reception but up on this floor all was quiet. Lady Enide had left Cat half an hour ago, with a smile of relief at the evening's success, and the boxes of jewellery Cat had worn.

Standing barefoot in the corridor, her hair loose around her shoulders, Cat should have felt nervous. Physical intimacy with Alex would make their inevitable parting more difficult. Yet a force stronger than logic drove her. After being constrained to do others' bidding, it was freeing to make her choice and act on it.

Crazy to think she'd known him less than two weeks. He'd changed her irrevocably.

Or had she changed herself? Had coming here, taking the chance to connect with the part of her life she'd always denied, made a difference?

Cat had lived cautiously, every step planned, always on the defensive, never taking big risks. It felt glorious now to follow the voice of instinct, not caution.

She raised her hand again but, instead of knocking, she turned the handle and walked in, closing the door behind her.

Mellow lamplight spilled across the sitting room and a gauzy curtain riffled at an open door. Swiftly Cat crossed to the door then paused, her heart too big in her chest, as she took in the tall, broad-shouldered man standing there in the gloom of the balcony.

In the distance a final car rolled away down the gravelled drive and the high gates swung shut behind it.

'The Prime Minister has left.' Alex swung round, the play of shadows casting his face in stark lines. 'He wasn't happy.'

'Not happy?' Cat hesitated. She didn't want to talk about politicians. 'The evening was a huge success.'

'In more ways than one.' Alex opened his arms. 'Come here.' Cat didn't respond well to orders, but this one, in a husky baritone that sent delicious ripples down her backbone, was different.

Wordlessly she went to him. His arms folded her

close and then his mouth was on hers, urgent, almost rough, as he leaned into her, prising her willing lips open, delving deep as if he hadn't eaten in a month and she was a banquet laid out for his delectation.

Cat wound her arms around his shoulders, swaying back in his arms as he bent over her. His thick hair was soft to the touch, his hard thighs hot against hers and the taste of him drove her wild.

'I thought you'd never come.' He nipped a line of kisses down her throat and wildfire flared. Her nipples tightened and puckered as she pressed herself against him.

'I had to get changed.'

A possessive hand stroked the silk of her robe from shoulder to thigh, then slipped round to clasp her buttock and haul her against him.

Cat gasped as she came in contact with his erection. It had only been days but it felt like a lifetime since she'd felt him against her, inside her.

'I thought you were beautiful in that ball gown, but I prefer you like this.' His hand captured the back of her head. 'You've let your hair down too.'

Cat opened her mouth to ask if he preferred it that way, but got her answer when he took her mouth again. His kiss was urgent, hungry, like the press of his body and the iron-hard arm lashing her to him.

Where they touched fire kindled and blazed. Every sense went on alert as she began to spiral into mindless delight. The small night sounds grew distant, eclipsed by their breathing and the throb of her pulse in her ears. Already her body was softening for him.

It took everything Cat had to tear her mouth away.

'Wait.' Her voice was an almost silent gasp yet he heard. She felt a tremor pass through his big, lean body then he stilled.

'Second thoughts?'

Cat leaned back in his arms, enough to see the too-tight clench of his jaw and the frown lining his brow. It struck her that, even now, Alex would pull back if she changed her mind. Her chest tightened. She touched his forehead, smoothing the crinkles with unsteady fingers.

'No.'

The instant relief on his features would have been balm to her ego except Cat couldn't relax yet. She had one last hurdle to face. A shadow that threatened to dull her joy.

'Cat? What's wrong?' His voice was sharp.

'We need to talk.' She shook her head. 'Things aren't as simple as you think.'

'Simple? Nothing about this situation is simple. Except that we want each other.' He paused, holding her gaze. 'Don't we, Cat?'

There was challenge in his tone, and something else. If she didn't know better, she'd think Alex nervous.

'Yes.'

His lips stopped speech and the taste of him, the warmth of his arms holding her, made her knees crumple.

Reluctantly she put her palms on his chest and stepped back on wobbly legs. He loosened his hold just enough that a sliver of chilly night air passed between them.

Alex stared down at that determined chin and froze. She couldn't deny him. Not now.

He could ignore her doubts and seduce her. From the first there'd been one truth neither of them could deny—the phenomenal, unstoppable attraction they shared. Cat went up in flames when they kissed.

Except he didn't want anything coming between them this time. Whatever the problem, he'd deal with it. He wanted Cat and he'd have her, no matter what it took.

'What's wrong? Is it the Prime Minister?'

Cat blinked up at him, a little befuddled, and satisfaction filled him. She wasn't as in control as she pretended. Did she realise her hands were roving his chest? That slow caress made him want to return the favour. The thought of his hands on her sweet breasts dragged heat through his groin and he stiffened.

'You don't need to worry about him.' Alex's voice was rough. 'He left tonight thinking you'd fooled me, so you've fulfilled your contract.' He paused, thinking of the satisfaction he'd derive later, once Cat was safely away from here. Then Alex would deal properly with the man who'd schemed to deceive him.

'I did happen to mention, though, that there'd be no royal match.' It had been small compensation, seeing the man's hopes crumble—all those machinations for nothing.

Cat shivered in his hold. 'He won't like that.'

Alex drew her close. This time she didn't resist and unfamiliar emotion filled him when she met his eyes. Delight and protectiveness and something more.

'I won't let him hurt you, Cat.'

'It's not up to you to protect me. I can do that.' Then her mouth curved in that unstinting smile that made him catch his breath. 'But thank you; I appreciate it.'

'So if he's not the problem, what is?' He slipped his hand through her hair, drawing the silky threads back, watching her eyelids lower and her head tilt in sensual appreciation.

How he wanted her! From the crown of her head to her dainty feet that could fell a man with one kick. He wanted her passion and her smiles. Even the way her smooth brow knotted when she was troubled, her pride and strength when she faced things that made her nervous. The way her jaw angled, ready to argue. He wanted it all.

'I need to tell you about myself.' There it was, that clear-eyed, almost defiant look that he'd learned could hide nerves as well as determination.

'Can't it wait?'

'No. I don't want to keep anything from you. You need to know this first.'

That word *first* held a promise that made his heart race. Whatever Cat's problem, it was something more than nerves at not being able to dance or hold her own discussing science. Her whole body was tense.

Alex stilled, all except his hand, gently soothing her. 'Go on.'

'You asked who I was and I told you.' She paused and drew in a deep breath. 'What I didn't tell you is that Dubois was my stepfather. My mother was pregnant to someone else when they married.'

Alex nodded. So her biological father hadn't been a baker in a provincial town. Somehow it didn't surprise him.

'My real father was the King of St Galla. Amelie's father. I'm her bastard half-sister.'

That explained the remarkable similarity between them. Now it all made sense! He'd thought a cousin, but this—

'Why don't you say something?' The razor edge to her words caught his attention. In the dim light she looked pale and strained.

'Thank you for telling me. I imagine not many know.'

'No one. Though Enide guessed.' She watched him intently as if expecting more.

'Did he mistreat you? Your stepfather?'

Cat tilted her head as if to view him better. 'He was a bully who wasn't afraid to use his hands. He was bitter that my mother never gave him children of his own, and resentful of harbouring someone else's bastard even though he'd been well paid to marry my mother. Because he made his distaste clear, everyone else despised us too.'

There it was again. *Bastard.* Why not say 'illegitimate'? Or 'natural daughter'? It was as if Cat chose the most brutal description she could.

'I'm sorry.' He cuddled her close. 'No child should have to experience that.'

Now he began to understand. She'd been rejected by both the King and the man paid...*paid* to be her father! No wonder Cat held herself apart from everyone else.

It explained too, her early interest in self-defence.

His jaw tightened as he thought of her as a kid, ostracised in her own town and needing lessons to defend herself against her stepfather.

'I'm not looking for sympathy.'

Of course she wasn't. She was so fiercely independent Alex wondered if she'd ever leaned on anyone. It moved him that she'd confided in him. Would she turn to him if ever she needed help?

'You're not surprised?'

He shrugged. 'I guessed there was some close connection between the two of you.'

'And now you know?'

What did she want him to say? 'Did you ever meet your birth father?'

Cat shook her head. 'I was his dirty little secret. I never met him or his family.'

Her family too. Suddenly, urgently, Alex wanted to hold her close and never release her.

'I thought you needed to know the truth about me.'

'I'm glad you trust me enough to tell me.'

'Because if anyone guessed my true identity there'd be an uproar.'

Alex peered down into her set expression. '*That's* what's bothering you?'

'I'm a potential embarrassment to you and to Amelie for that matter.'

Alex stared. She was warning him off? She thought he cared so much for gossip? The idea pricked his pride. 'Amelie can look after herself and so can I.'

'You don't care?'

'I care that both the men who should have loved and protected you betrayed you. I care that your childhood was difficult and that you seem to expect rejection as a matter of course.' He lifted his hand to her cheek and felt her lashes flutter. 'I care that you think it would make any difference to us.'

'Alex?' Her voice was a raw whisper, so bewildered it sent something like grief scything through him.

'Is there anything else I need to know?'

'Isn't that enough?' Her voice cracked.

'Yes. I've had enough conversation.' He tucked his arms under her, lifted her against his chest and stalked into the sitting room. He intended to prove to her that not all men were as selfish as the ones she'd known.

Passing into the darkened bedroom he paused, giving his eyes time to adjust.

'You're sure about this?' Cat's voice feathered his neck.

He laughed, the sound too tight. 'I've never been more sure of anything. I need you, Cat. And unless you tell me you've changed your mind I intend to spend the night making love to you.'

He lay her on the bed and settled next to her hip, looking down into wide, solemn eyes. 'I need you too, Alex.' She reached for his shoulders and tugged.

But, instead of lowering himself to her, Alex made himself stay where he was. Already tension was razor-sharp. Lying against her, even fully clothed, he wouldn't trust himself not to lose control.

He tugged the tie at her waist then peeled open her robe, first one side then the other, revealing tip-tilted breasts and fluid planes and curves that invited his touch.

'Take your clothes off, Alex.'

'Not yet.' He leaned down, kissing one darkened nipple that trembled at his touch. His tongue slipped out, circling it, tasting her unique, sweet flavour. He had to plant his hands wide on the bed on either side of her, so as not to touch. If he touched he'd be lost.

She cradled him with both hands, tugging him close, and he gave in to her silent pleas to suckle at her breast. Desire jolted, solid as a blade to his belly. His erection grew impossibly harder and he had to take a moment to gather his shredding control.

'Alex, I want you.' Her siren whisper curled around him, inviting him to release. But he wanted to treasure her, show Cat he cared enough to give without taking—yet. Show her she was important. He hadn't realised how important till she'd told him about her identity and her past and he'd wanted to do violence to someone for the pain she'd suffered.

He let his hand trail down her ribs, past her navel to the softness of her belly and lower, to the V of rough silk between her legs. Instantly her thighs parted and her sigh scattered his thoughts.

She was slick and needy, shifting with every minuscule circling of his thumb. When he probed deeper her hips jerked and she gasped his name in a sound that was part purr, part protest.

With one last lick at her breast he sat back, watching her hands drop to the bedspread and clench the fabric as his caress between her thighs deepened. Her eyes were closed and her lips open as if she couldn't get enough air.

He'd never seen anything so erotic in his life.

'Look at me, Cat. Open your eyes.' Finally they opened, slowly as if it took enormous effort. Alex smiled. He could grow addicted to the sight of Cat's pleasure. 'Now watch me.'

Spreading her knees with his palms, he settled himself between her legs and stroked her with his tongue. She would have shot off the bed but for the weight of his arms and shoulders forcing her down.

'Alex! Please! I want you.'

Her voice was a potent aphrodisiac and he had

to pause, conjuring a mathematical equation to distract himself from the urgent need to shuck off his clothes and plunge into her.

'Soon.' The word was muffled against her body as he licked where his fingers had traced. She shuddered and shifted. Alex smiled as he caressed her with his hand and his mouth till he felt her tremble and she sobbed. Strong hands gripped him and her knees came up as the storm broke upon her. On and on it went, Alex gladly feeding it with deft caresses till, with a guttural cry, she collapsed back.

He lifted himself to survey her, a tumble of lithe limbs, hair splayed in waves across the bedding. She was the picture of abandoned sensuality but she was more too. That curious, too-tight feeling was back, as if his ribs had contracted against his heart and lungs. He wanted her but he wanted more too. He—

'Alex. Please. Come here.'

Gingerly, aware of the needy throb of his erection against tailored trousers that no longer seemed to fit, he moved up the bed to lie on his side next to her. Somewhere along the line he'd kicked his shoes off but otherwise he was fully clothed, his bow tie choking him. Propped on one elbow, he reefed the tie loose then began to open his shirt.

Movement tickled his abdomen. Cat, nimbly dealing with the fastening of his trousers.

'Not yet.' The brush of her hands there was delicate torture. But she was quicker than he'd imagined. A moment later a strong, slender leg curved round his waist and a hand tugged his shoulder, pulling him off balance so his weight rested on her.

Another slender leg rose to clamp his waist, tugging him down as she lifted her pelvis.

Stars sprinkled the blackness behind his closed lids as he tried to breathe through the tsunami of sensation. She'd undone his clothes enough so that, as she rose to him, he rested right at her centre. She rose again and fire trailed through his groin and exploded in his blood.

He'd meant to wait. He'd planned to give her climax after climax before satisfying himself.

'Open your eyes, Alex. Open them and look at me.' Her throaty voice was irresistible and he found himself snared by the sight of her. Another deliberate, slow lift of her hips and he couldn't help himself. With a groan of surrender he pushed his clothes out of the way, tilted his hips and slid down, down, right to her heart.

The world stopped. Even, he'd swear, the blood in his arteries paused for a second.

Cat's smile of triumph was short-lived when he took control, one hand planted on the bed, the other sliding beneath her, lifting her to him. She gasped as gravity fitted them even tighter together.

The sensations threatened to slay him. Especially when he leaned in and kissed her breast, tasting her again.

'Alex!' She grabbed his arms, eyes widening, and he felt the tremors of her climax around him. The world trembled and, with a roar of triumph, he spilled himself.

Through it all he held her eyes, and her shuddering body, and knew he never wanted to be anywhere else.

CHAPTER THIRTEEN

CAT HUMMED AS she packed. The day had dawned grey and wet, first sign of the winter that had already settled on the mainland peaks. But that couldn't dim her happiness.

She'd finish packing then cancel her flight to New York. Alex had invited her to Bengaria. She was nervous about visiting his home but she'd grasp what he offered with both hands.

Last night she'd realised why his trust mattered so much. Why she'd had to tell him about herself. Why she was taking risks she'd never dared take before.

She loved him.

She'd known him less than two weeks but she loved him!

Waking beside Alex, she'd realised what she wanted most was to wake beside him every day for the rest of her life. To share her life and be an integral part of his.

He'd taken the news of her identity better than

she'd hoped, but the chances of a permanent relationship…?

A shiver raced down her spine but she ignored it. The die was cast—she couldn't change her feelings—so she'd grasp happiness while she could and worry about tomorrow later.

She'd never been in love, never known any love but her mother's and that had been overshadowed by her bullying stepfather who'd made their lives hell.

Fierce joy eclipsed Cat's fear. For once she'd embrace life rather than insulating herself against it. Soon too she'd meet Amelie, the sister she'd never known. She'd never felt so excited.

Someone tapped on her door and her heart lifted. 'Come in!' She was hurrying across, expecting Alex, when the door opened.

'Enide? What's wrong?' The other woman looked terrible, her face grey. She clasped her hands in front of her and leaned back against the door for support.

Cat stared. Despite her age the old lady usually held herself ramrod-straight, her posture perfect.

'Are you all right? Please, take a seat.'

Enide shook her head. 'There's no time.' Her gaze took in the suitcase. 'You're almost packed.

Excellent. Your flight to New York has been brought forward.'

'I'm not going to New York. I'm flying to—'

'Bengaria?'

'How did you know?' Cat looked at Enide's pinched mouth and foreboding slithered through her. 'Please, sit down. I'm worried about you.'

For a second the older woman's expression softened but the impression was gone in a blink.

'There's no time. The Prime Minister has ordered a private jet to take you to New York.'

'But I'm going to—'

'Bengaria? I'm afraid not. King Alex's plans have altered.' She drew herself higher. 'He's staying here to deal with a crisis. The last thing he needs is to be seen with you.' Enide wrung her hands. 'I saw the attraction between you but I didn't for one moment think—'

'What's happened, Enide?' Cat's belly roiled. She took the older woman by the arm and gently helped her to a seat. 'You're worrying me. Do you want a glass of water? A—?'

'Nothing.' Enide shook her head.

Cat wanted to scream in frustration. Her nerves stretched to breaking point. 'Tell me. Please!'

'There were paparazzi at the gate last night, photographing guests.'

That was expected. Photographers had pointed cameras at the royal limousine when she and Alex went to the city.

'One of them stayed after the ball finished. As if he knew it would be worthwhile.' Enide's gaze turned piercing.

'I don't understand. Can't you please explain?'

After a moment Enide nodded. 'I believe you. I told myself you weren't devious. You didn't organise this.'

'Organise what?' Cat glanced at the door. Maybe it would be faster finding Alex.

'Photos have been delivered to the palace—photos taken with a telephoto lens, of you and Alex on his balcony, kissing. Of him carrying you into his suite. It's obvious you're wearing nothing beneath your robe, and you're *not* talking affairs of state.'

Cat tottered to the bed and sank onto it. Photos of her and Alex? While they'd talked, kissed... While she'd shared the truth about herself and fallen even more in love with the man who'd accepted that revelation as if it was nothing...

All that time someone had been watching, photographing?

Cat shivered, hunching her shoulders and rubbing her hands over her arms.

'I feel sick.' She wanted to scrub herself under a hot shower to alleviate the feeling of violation. She'd seen Afra like this last year, when stalked by a crazed fan. Cat had sympathised and thought she'd understood. But nothing prepared her for this sick sensation of helplessness.

She lifted her head and read distress in Enide's eyes. 'Has Alex seen the photos?'

'They were sent to him too, with a request for an exclusive interview. The implication is that if there's no interview they'll be posted publicly.'

Cat pressed her hand to her churning stomach. 'This is a nightmare.' She stared at the carpet, the trailing pattern of gold on ivory, and a thought struck her dazed brain. Her head jerked up. 'They think I'm Amelie. That it was Alex and Amelie...'

Enide's nod confirmed the worst. 'I suppose I should blame you for putting Amelie in an untenable position. But I can't in all honesty blame you. This situation has been fraught from the start. And Alex is a particularly charming man.' Her mouth trembled. 'I just can't see a way out of this mess for either you or Amelie.'

'I have to make a statement. Explain.' How had

something so wondrous and beautiful turned into disaster?

'No! That's exactly what we don't need. Bad enough that the paparazzi believe they have proof Amelie and Alex are in a relationship. We can't tell them what *really* happened. Amelie said she'll return soon and it's vital you're not here when she arrives.'

Cat shot to her feet, nervous energy filling her. 'But this needs to be set right.' Though how, she didn't know. She swayed as she thought of the fall-out for Alex and for Amelie. Neither wanted to be shackled to the other yet now everyone would believe—

'I must see Alex.'

'You can't. He's not here. He left as soon as he received the photos.' The older woman's mouth twisted. 'He looked like he wanted to do someone violence. He's convinced the Prime Minister is behind the photos, trying to force him into a royal marriage.'

Cat's jaw dropped. 'You think Alex would let himself be *blackmailed* into a dynastic marriage?'

'I don't know what to think. Except it's the sort of devious trick Barthe might pull. As for blackmail…it's no secret St Gallan money would be welcome in Bengaria. Alex needs investment for major projects he's negotiating. A pragmatic man could decide the scandal of publicly rejecting our Princess would be too costly.' She paused. 'If anyone can sort this out, Alex is the man.'

Cat swayed as the room spun. Alex and Amelie wouldn't marry if they didn't want to. Even for the good of their countries—the idea was too medieval. But Enide was right; Alex had intimated the business investment he was brokering on this visit was vital.

She put a hand to her whirling head. 'I need to see him. As soon as he returns to the palace.'

'I'm sorry, my dear. I suspect he won't be back for quite some time. Which may be as well.' Enide grimaced. 'He needs time to cool down. I've never seen a man so furious.'

Pain stabbed Cat's heart. 'He couldn't believe I had anything to do with it.'

Yet Cat had duped him once under the Prime Minister's orders. And only last night Alex had told the PM the marriage was off so maybe this *was* a strategic move by Barthe. If there was a plot to force Alex's hand, he'd have to wonder about her role.

Cat's skin grew clammy.

Deception was Alex's hot button. And while he'd spoken of liking and respecting her, she guessed for him their relationship was mainly about sex. She'd be mad to read anything more into his invitation to Bengaria.

'Did he mention me?' Cat saw Enide's sympathetic look but couldn't afford pride. She had to know.

'Not a word.'

Cat's stomach dropped. She swung around and fumbled for her phone. Alex had given her his private number. Surely once they spoke—

She dialled. After two rings she got the answerphone. It hadn't gone straight there though. He must have seen who was calling and declined the call.

The phone fell from numb fingers as Cat's hopes shattered.

Alex had forgiven her once. But he'd never allow himself to be duped twice. Clearly he believed she'd been part of a scam to force his hand.

She stumbled, bracing herself on the wall as despair engulfed her.

A knock sounded and Cat's head came up, her heart slamming high in her chest. *Alex!*

'I'm sorry, my dear, but that's your escort to the

plane. I'm afraid I don't have the authority to intervene.' The old lady looked so distressed Cat found herself nodding, her chest aching.

'It's okay.' She forced her lips into a grim smile. 'Once I talk to Alex we'll sort something out.' If she said it often enough she might believe it.

Enide opened the door to a pair of grim-faced men Cat recognised from the Prime Minister's security team.

So that was it. She wasn't being given a chance to see Alex. She could evade the two guards but there'd be more nearby. She couldn't outmanoeuvre them all.

Defeat hollowed her belly. She wanted to fight for herself and Alex, for what they'd so briefly shared. Yet how could she if Alex refused to listen?

It took thirty-five minutes to get to the private jet. Thirty-five minutes and sixteen calls to Alex's private line.

Each time she got the answer machine.

He was blocking her calls.

There wasn't even a two-word text saying he'd call later.

She remembered his words. More, she remembered the soft savagery in his voice. *'No one fools me more than once. When my trust is betrayed that's the end.'*

Cat crossed her arms tight across her chest as the plane hurtled down the runway, as if she could hold back the heart threatening to burst from her chest. The pain was so intense every breath hurt. Even thinking hurt.

Alex had decided she was guilty.

There'd be no second chance.

CHAPTER FOURTEEN

'CAT, ARE YOU OKAY?' Afra's eyes caught hers in the limo's rear-view mirror.

'Isn't it my job to ask you that?' Cat forced a smile, glancing at the chauffeur beside her. The guy had been surprised when she'd insisted on sitting up front. But she was Afra's bodyguard, not a VIP.

'You look tense.' Afra's voice didn't sound right.

Cat pushed her shoulders down, realising they'd inched up towards her ears. Tense was right. Tense and sick with nerves. How had she let herself be persuaded to accompany Afra on this extra stage of her new tour?

'Everything's fine.' *That* was how Cat had been persuaded—because Afra was still nervous after the horror of last year's stalker. If it weren't for that Cat would have refused point-blank to visit Bengaria, even if it was for a single benefit concert.

'It's a pretty city.' She turned to survey a cobble-stoned square and charming old buildings. Despite the chill there were lots of people walking and cycling, enjoying the sunny Saturday.

Cat wished she were anywhere else in the world but here, in Bengaria's capital. It had only been ten days since she'd left Alex in St Galla and she felt stretched too thin by the enormity of her loss.

As if she'd ever really had a chance of a meaningful relationship with him!

Her nerves were shredded, waiting for the press furore to start when those tell-tale photos were published. So far they hadn't hit the media. Maybe they wouldn't. Maybe instead there'd be an announcement of a royal wedding.

Nausea cramped her belly.

'Hold on.' Her voice cracked as she pivoted to the driver, alert for danger. 'We're going the wrong way. This isn't the way to the concert hall.' Cat might never have been here but she'd learned the route by heart.

'Sorry. I forgot to tell you.' There it was again, that wobble in Afra's voice. 'There was a last-minute change. We're at a new venue.'

The hairs at Cat's nape lifted as they turned into a wide boulevard and she saw a massive building at the end of an avenue of trees. 'Afra?' She had a *really* bad feeling.

In the mirror their eyes met and Cat knew instantly she'd been conned. Afra wasn't afraid for her life, but she *was* on edge.

'Tell me.' Cat's voice was terse, her short nails digging into the palms of her hand.

'I'm performing at the palace. After all, it's for a charity sponsored by the royal family.'

Cat was still struggling to swallow the burning knot of tangled emotion blocking her throat when they swept through ornate wrought iron gates. A troop of royal guards marched by, the absolute precision of their movements as eye-catching as their ceremonial uniform of sky-blue tunics, tall fur hats and dark trousers.

Numb, she looked up to the huge grey palace before her and saw the Bengarian flag flying proud. The King was in residence.

Cat stood on the edge of the room, eyes flicking from the singer who'd performed for the Dowager Queen's charity, to the crowd filling the Mirrored Hall.

She stood out from the other women, in a black tailored jacket, low heels and slim trousers. There was no glint of jewellery at her throat or ears to draw a glance, yet Alex couldn't take his eyes off her.

Her pale hair glowed under the light of the Venetian glass chandeliers. It was drawn back from her face, falling in waves, and he wanted to reach out and touch it. He recalled the soft stroke of it on his bare flesh as they made love. The scent of it...

Hell, every detail of the time they'd spent together was indelibly tattooed on his brain. Including her vulnerable expression as she'd told him about her birth father and waited for rejection.

He'd *known* that and yet he'd been so swept up in fury that last morning he'd thought of nothing but stopping those photos. By the time he'd realised his mistake it was too late. The damage was done and Cat was gone.

She'd *run* rather than face him! An unholy brew of indignation, pain and guilt stirred in his belly.

Alex stalked towards her, grateful her attention was on Afra. Not once in the hour and a half since she'd arrived had Cat's eyes met his. Every time he looked at her she was busy scanning the crowd or checking on the singer, intent, it seemed, on everything but him.

She couldn't have made it more obvious that she didn't want to see him.

'Ms Dubois.'

She spun round, eyes wide. His heart catapulted in his chest. What was she thinking? More important—what did she *feel*?

Before she could retreat he took her hand. Instantly she froze, all except the runaway pulse fluttering at her wrist. A pulse that gave him hope after ten long days of regret and uncertainty.

Alex was tempted to kiss her hand but he needed all his focus. Kissing Cat, even the back of her hand, would be too distracting.

'Come. We need to talk.'

Of course she resisted, pulling back, but he didn't let her break his hold.

'I'm working.' Her tone was cool.

'You're relieved of duty.' He nodded to the two security men who'd followed him. Silently they positioned themselves, their focus on Afra. 'Your employer has accepted my offer of protection while in Bengaria. You're off-duty.'

'You can't—'

'I can and will.' He leaned in, inhaling her delicious perfume. 'Don't fight me, Cat, unless you *want* to make a public spectacle.'

Her mouth opened then closed. Fire blazed in her green eyes. 'Five minutes.'

Alex nodded and led her away. This would take more than five minutes. And if at the end she wasn't convinced? A vice clamped his lungs. He refused to consider that.

Her face was blank when he invited her to take a seat in his private chambers.

'No, thanks. I prefer to stand.'

Alex raked a hand through his hair. She wasn't going to make this easy, was she?

'You ran.' They weren't the words he'd planned, but that sharp tug of pain in his gut made them spill out.

'I didn't run. I left for New York as planned.'

'Not as planned.' He paced to the window, not seeing the view beyond. 'You'd agreed to come here with me.' Despite guilt at the poor way he'd handled things, it *hurt* that she'd left like that. 'I've never invited any other woman.'

He swung round and caught her stunned expression. 'It was obviously the only option.'

'Obviously? What about staying with me till we sorted everything out?'

'The way you stayed with me?' Her lip curled

and, despite the jarring blow to his conscience, Alex applauded her spirit.

'I apologise for that. I—'

'Apology accepted. Now, if you'll excuse me—'

His hand shot out, capturing hers. 'We're not done.'

For an instant her eyes gleamed bright as lasers, then the fire in them was eclipsed, her face washed of emotion. Alex hated watching it.

'Please, Cat. Let me explain.'

She swallowed hard and he wanted to wrap his arms around her and not let go. 'I apologise. I shouldn't have left the palace that morning without speaking to you. I was just so incensed.'

'I understand. You had a right to be. I was.' Except her voice told him anger was the least of her emotions. She was hurting too.

His lungs compressed so tight he couldn't breathe.

When he found his voice it didn't sound like him. 'It's my weak point. With anything else I'm slow to anger, but when it's deliberate trickery...' He heaved in a deep breath. 'That's no excuse but you need to understand.'

'I understand.' Still that bleak expression. 'You thought I'd set you up.'

'No!' His grip tightened on her hand. 'That's not why I left. I went to see the St Gallan Prime Minister.'

'Because you thought I was in cahoots with him.' She tugged her hand free and loss engulfed him.

'I went to *protect* you!' He'd never known such anger as when he realised Cat had been the unwitting victim of such a brutally intrusive scheme. He remembered how vulnerable she'd been that night, baring her past, and how strong. It had wrenched his heart to think of anyone callously using her that way. His concern for her outweighed outrage at the invasion of his own privacy.

'You wouldn't be able to shrug off those photos if they appeared in print.' Her expression confirmed it. 'Not when eventually people would dig till they discovered your real identity.'

Cat stared up at him and Alex felt a glimmer of hope. 'I realised too late that I should have stayed and spoken with you first, but I saw red and I acted.'

She shook her head. 'You rejected my calls.'

'I was in a meeting with the Prime Minister. I planned to contact you as soon as I could tell you everything was sorted and you had nothing to worry about. I wanted to fix everything.'

'But you didn't. You didn't call.'

Alex spread his hands. He wasn't used to having someone call him on his every action. 'I got it wrong. Later, when I saw the number of missed calls, I knew I needed to speak to you in person. But you'd left the palace.'

It had been clear then that it was too late to convince Cat. She'd made up her mind and who could blame her? More drastic measures were needed.

'But still you didn't call.' Hurt rang behind the challenge and his heart squeezed.

'I tried, but by then you'd switched off. What I had to say was too important for a message. I had to *see* you. See you somewhere you couldn't simply walk away without hearing me out. That's why this elaborate set-up—because I needed a home ground advantage.' In his more desperate moments he'd even wondered about kidnapping her, long enough to make her listen.

'I brought you here to explain and apologise.' But her stony expression worried him. 'I didn't think you'd set me up, Cat. That's what you believed, isn't it?' It was there in her bruised eyes and tight mouth.

'Of course you did. It was an obvious conclusion, even if it was wrong.'

'I never for a second believed you knew about the photos. I remember what we talked about out there on the balcony, Cat. What passed between us was too intimate, too real.' It had *moved* him. He'd never felt so connected to anyone as he had to Cat that night. Surely she'd felt the same.

He reached for her hand and read doubt in her eyes. Then she moved back a step and frustration rose.

'It doesn't matter now. Somehow you've managed to stop those pictures hitting the press so there's nothing more to talk about.'

'Nothing to talk about? What about us, Cat? Or did that mean so little to you?'

So little? Her breath snagged on a shard of pure pain. *If only.* Being in the same room was testing her to the limit. What did he *want* from her?

'How did you stop the photos being published, Alex?' Even saying his name was a forbidden delight. She shivered, wrapping her arms across her chest.

Alex mirrored her movements. On him the action emphasised his powerful male splendour. In formal clothes he was spectacular and she couldn't help drinking him in. This would be the last time she saw him. Once he got over his pique at her leaving. Because she knew now she couldn't survive what could only ever be a short fling for him. Even if he'd arranged today just to see her. Part of her was flattered, dangerously flattered.

'I told the Prime Minister to publish the photos and be damned.' Alex held her gaze, his strong chin thrust forward. 'I told him I had nothing to be ashamed of, being with the woman I intend to make my bride.'

Cat rocked back on her feet.

She'd half expected it but nothing had prepared her for hearing the words.

Alex intended to marry Amelie! They must have overcome their doubts about the marriage. After all, arranged marriages were common in royal circles, weren't they?

'Cat? Don't you have anything to say?'

Alex had moved closer. So close he loomed over her. There was nowhere else to look but into those stunning indigo eyes.

Cat tried to turn but her feet were cemented to the spot. She blinked and felt heat sear the back of her eyeballs.

'I hope you'll both be very happy.'

'Cat, did you hear what I said?' The deep resonance of his voice was like a touch trailing along her bare skin.

'Yes!' Anger vied with despair that he could affect her this way, even as he told her he was marrying her sister. 'You and Amelie are getting married and—'

Strong hands grabbed her elbows, hauling her up on her toes against him. Heat swamped her. Longing, confusion and shame that she couldn't conquer her feelings for him.

'It's you I want to marry, Cat!'

'What?'

She was drowning in sensation, revelling in his hard body against hers. Even the scent of his skin sent her hormones into overdrive.

'I told the St Gallan Prime Minister I was going to marry you. And that if those photos hit the press I'd immediately reveal you weren't Princess Amelie but my fiancée. I'd let it be known he'd tried to fool not just me but the people of St Galla by hiring an imposter.' He paused, his chest rising and dipping.

'It was a calculated risk. I know you didn't want your role there revealed but I couldn't see any other option. But I was right. He agreed to stop the release of the photos. He's about to announce his resignation, by the way. He was made to see he couldn't continue as Prime Minister.'

Cat gawked. She was stuck back on Alex wanting to marry her. 'You didn't have to say that, about marriage.'

'Why not? It's what I want. What I hope you want too.'

The world tilted abruptly and she swayed. Instantly Alex scooped her up against his chest.

'Put me down.'

'So you can faint at my feet?' Was that a hint of a smile?

'I'm not going to faint.' She should hate his managing attitude, carrying her as if she weighed nothing.

'Not while I'm holding you.' He sank onto a couch, still holding her close. Cat thought about breaking free but somehow couldn't find the willpower.

'Please, Alex. What do you want? Really?'

Instantly he sobered. 'You, Cat. I want you.'

'But we were just having an affair—'

His mouth covered hers and the world stopped spinning. Cat lost herself in the most perfect, sensuous yet gentle kiss of her life. When he lifted his lips she clung to him.

'What did I tell you, Cat? Do you remember? This is more than sex.'

'You said it was attraction. Desire. Respect. Liking.'

Alex grinned down at her and she'd swear she heard music playing and chimes ringing. 'You *did* listen! What do you think all that adds up to? *I love you, Cat.*'

The shock of it shuddered through her. How she wanted to believe. But miracles didn't happen. Cat lived in the real world, not some dreamland.

'You can't. We barely know each other.'

Instantly he sobered. 'I know everything I need to understand I want to be with you.' He paused. 'How do you feel about me? I thought you felt the same.'

'It doesn't matter what I feel.' She choked down the need to tell him she loved him. 'You're a king and I'm—'

'The woman I adore.'

She shut her eyes. It was too much, too tempting. 'I'm the illegitimate daughter of a king. I'm a scandal waiting to explode if you let me into your world.'

Alex's hand was warm as it cupped her face. 'I don't care. Nor does my mother.'

'Your mother?' It was close to a shriek.

'How do you think I managed today? It's her

charity event. And, for the record, I don't give a damn who your parents were. All I care about is you. Times have changed and Bengaria has changed with it. You'll see. I can marry anyone I want. Yes, your identity would be news but that would fade with time. We'd ride it out together.'

Cat shook her head. 'I won't marry you.'

'But you love me?'

Maybe a stronger woman would have denied it. But it was impossible for Cat when she saw his bravado hid a worried man.

'Of course I love you. I fell for you like a ton of bricks.'

This time Alex's kiss was so thorough that when it ended her hair was loose, his tie had disappeared and they were both breathing heavily. Pleasure engulfed her. Not just pleasure but the warm glow of love.

'Tell me again.' His lips grazed her ear and she shivered.

'I love you, Alex. But I can't marry you.'

He pulled back and pinioned her with his darkening gaze. 'One thing at a time. You love me. That's what counts. And you'll come and live here in Bengaria, won't you? I can't promise it will be all balls and parties. I've got years of hard work ahead, but I promise I'll do everything I can to make you happy here.'

Give up her life and her job to live here? As what? His mistress? His girlfriend? The old Cat, the one who'd never known love or risk, would have said no.

'Please, Cat. I want to spend my life with you. I want to share your life too. Always. Together. Give us a chance.'

His words were a perfect reflection of her own desires. They made her heart turn over.

'It's mad. We've only known each other—'

'Twenty-one days.'

She shook her head, trying hard not to respond to the smile curling his firm lips and failing. 'For ten of those we've been on separate continents.'

He nodded gravely. 'I blame you for that. You've got a lot of making up to do, Ms Dubois.' His hand moved, stroking down her side and around to pull her up against him. Arousal jolted through her and she arched into him.

'Say you'll move to Bengaria, sweetheart. I have connections.' He winked. 'I'm sure you can get a visa to work here.'

Her laughter covered the emotion choking her throat. 'You'd be seen dating a bodyguard?'

'So long as dating means I get to do this.' He

kissed his way down from her mouth, grazing his teeth on the erogenous zone at the base of her neck, drawing her to breathless anticipation.

Alex drew back. 'I've found a place on the edge of the capital that might make an excellent youth centre. You'd have to check it, but if not there we'll find somewhere else.'

His expression made her heart dance. 'I've contacted young Thomas's new foster parents too. They've promised to bring him here for the opening, if you decide to go ahead. I thought you'd like a little St Gallan support.'

Cat stared, unable to take it in. 'You did all that? Really?'

He grabbed her hand and kissed her palm. Cat melted.

'Whatever it takes to make you happy. I want to marry you but I understand you're not sure. We'll take things as slowly as you like. As long as you're with me, that's what matters.'

Cat lifted her hand to his jaw, revelling in the feel of his clean-shaven skin stretched over strong bone, in the thrill of being here, with him, but most of all in the love she saw in his eyes.

It was time to take the biggest risk of her life.

'I can't think of anything I'd like more.'

EPILOGUE

CAT SMOOTHED A hand down the bronze silk of her ball gown. Outside fresh snow dusted the picturesque city but in the Mirrored Hall it was warm enough for a sleeveless dress. Alex's face when he'd seen her in it confirmed she'd chosen well.

'Shall we, Ms Dubois?' Alex stood before her, wearing a jacket of indigo and black trousers with an indigo side stripe—the dress uniform of his old regiment.

He was Prince Charming, except that knowing smile and the lascivious gleam in his eyes didn't belong in a children's story. Was he remembering why they'd almost been late for their own engagement ball? Fire fizzed in her blood. Even after months their passion was strong. Their love grew each day.

'Thank you, Your Highness.' Cat let him lead her to the centre of the room and the orchestra struck up a familiar tune. The 'Emperor Waltz'.

Suddenly the enormous changes in her life hit

her. From imposter to almost royal. From alone to loved and cherished. Cat met Alex's intent gaze and smiled with all her heart.

He hauled her to him, his embrace warm and strong.

'Aren't you holding me too close?'

Alex shook his head, his expression suddenly serious. 'I want the world to know I love you. You've made me happier than I thought possible.'

As he'd made her. They spent as much time as possible together and Alex didn't keep anything from her. The highs and lows of his work. The challenges ahead. And he supported her as she painstakingly built the youth centre she'd dreamed of so long.

Together they'd faced the press and the Bengarian people. It wasn't easy but her adopted country had opened its arms to her, presumably because Alex was so obviously happy. After the flurry of headlines when, with Amelie's support, her identity was officially announced, the media was surprisingly positive. Most put an upbeat spin on the long-lost sister angle and the whirlwind romance.

She'd even met her nephew and begun to establish a relationship with him.

'You've made me happy too.' Cat smiled up into

Alex's indigo eyes and seconds later was spinning and swaying, her skirts swishing around them as she clung tight and gazed up at the man who'd stolen her heart.

The ballroom was a swirling collection of snapshots. Alex's mother, elegant and smiling as she leaned close to Lady Enide. Alex's cousin, Marisa in vivid orange, beside her handsome Brazilian husband, Damaso. People she barely knew, wearing diadems and jewels. A sprinkling of friends from America, grinning.

Then, in a gown of pistachio-green, her sister Amelie, smiling. Beside her, inevitably, stood the big bear of a man who never seemed to take his eyes off her.

Cat had wondered what it was like to have family. Now she knew it was one of life's most precious gifts.

Almost as precious as the man holding her tight.

'Have I told you how much I adore you, Your Highness?' The words emerged husky with emotion.

Alex swung her to a stop in the centre of the floor, ignoring the music and their audience. 'Yes, but feel free to repeat yourself, darling Cat.'

Then his mouth claimed hers and the room receded till even the thunderous applause was eclipsed by Alex's kiss.

Cat knew, whatever the future held, she was home.

* * * * *

If you enjoyed
HIS MAJESTY'S TEMPORARY BRIDE,
look out for the second part of Annie West's
THE PRINCESS SEDUCTIONS *duet*

THE GREEK'S FORBIDDEN PRINCESS
Available March 2018!